BLOOM

JOANNE MARSAN

ISBN: 978-1-970179-15-6 | First Edition - September 2025

Book Project Management by Raindrop Creative, Inc. | StartWrite Publish Team

Editor: Tiara Brown

Cover Art: Donovan Purvey

DEDICATION

First and foremost, I would like to express my deepest gratitude to Marcus Gill for providing the opportunity and platform for authors like me to share our voices through published work.

Special thanks to Raindrop Creative Inc. for their support in bringing my vision to life–from editing to presentation, your contribution has been invaluable.

TABLE OF CONTENTS

CHAPTER 1
A Religious Childhood

Living in a home where peace was her ultimate goal, Anika Bailes, a twenty-year-old woman, had a bright future ahead of her. Full of potential, she excelled in drawing, singing, and helping others achieve their dreams. As a college student, Anika was deeply curious about people's lives. She strongly desired to guide them back on track when they strayed off course. Raised in the Great Samaritan Church culture, she was known as the quiet, kind-hearted girl who always sought to bring joy to others.

Anika grew up in a small town called The Valley on Bellevue Street. The name of the city might seem odd for Quebec, a predominantly French-speaking province in Canada, but The Valley had always been unique. Its multicultural roots stemmed from businesses and workers who had settled there from England and the United States generations ago.

Although The Valley wasn't the fanciest town in Quebec, it had its own charm. The local park, for instance, was a central attraction, beautifully maintained and bustling with activity. It was vast, with outdoor concerts for music lovers, rustic wooden benches for families enjoying picnics, and a small lake where ducks swam alongside vibrant fish. The park also featured numerous biking trails, perfect for outdoor enthusiasts. In autumn, colorful leaves fell gracefully to the ground, creating a magical scene. Children would gleefully play in piles of leaves while their parents watched, laughing at their joy.

Anika's neighborhood was always lively, with something happening almost every day. Near her home was a small mall, a popular hangout spot for the town's youth. The mall featured a cozy food court where students often gathered to study together, as well as a café section where friends could share moments over a warm cup of coffee.

Adjacent to the mall was the Great Samaritan Church—a landmark in the neighborhood. Its massive structure made it impossible for anyone driving by to miss. Its grand, towering structure dominated the skyline and served as a beacon for the entire society. Though the Great Samaritan Church may not be something you've heard of before, this community had strong beliefs. They believed in working diligently for six days and dedicating the seventh day entirely to rest—a day they called the Sabbath. Devoted Samaritans also placed great emphasis on maintaining good health, often advocating for a vegetarian or vegan lifestyle as part of their approach. The church wasn't just a building but a symbol of the community's unity; it was the heart of Anika's upbringing.

Likewise, Anika's grandparents and earlier ancestors had been pillars of the church. Anika's family was deeply rooted in the community. Her parents were well-known and highly respected, and their influence extended across generations. Everyone in town knew the family name and what it stood for–all thanks to her parents' unwavering dedication and active involvement in various ministries. In many ways, Anika's parents were the heart and soul of the church–figures beloved by all who had woven their lives into the very fabric of the city.

Her mother was especially beloved for her generous spirit and culinary talents. Every week, without fail, she would serve meals after the church service. Her contributions were a warm and comforting highlight for everyone. Affectionately known as "Mamoushka," a term that captured her nurturing nature and constant care for church members and others, Anika's mother was a source of joy to all who knew her. Despite having attended nursing school but never completing it, Anika's mother became a renowned cook. Her meals, prepared with love and attention to detail, were cherished by adults and children alike. Anika had never tasted anything better than her mother's hearty, flavorful dishes.

Anika's father, the church elder, was equally admired and relied upon. He was responsible for ensuring the church was well-stocked and that everything ran smoothly. His commitment to his duties was unquestionable, and he was often seen fixing equipment, chatting with churchgoers, or ensuring the church's needs were met. A man of great pride, Anika's father cherished his heritage–his own father and grandfather had served as pastors at the same church–and took immense pride in continuing that legacy. His love for people and his work were evident in every action he took, making him a steadfast and beloved presence in the congregation.

Anika's family home had been passed down through generations, a legacy from her grandparents. Despite its age, the house was in excellent condition–a testament to her family's tradition of keeping their surroundings clean and well-maintained. At home, Anika's family lived by a set of health principles that her mother regularly shared with the church. The "8 Laws of Health" were a guideline to healthy living that included eating right, exercising, getting enough sleep, soaking up vitamin D, and practicing temperance. Concepts like this were what Anika had grown up hearing. The emphasis was on living in harmony with both body and spirit.

While these ideals may have seemed like sound advice to many, Anika found them challenging to embrace. She wasn't fond of the vegetarian or vegan lifestyle. Additionally, the contradictions didn't stop there. Anika's mother, a strong advocate for healthy living, often indulged in chocolate bars late at night and then complained about gaining weight. "*Talk about healthy living!?*" Anika would think, noticing the irony.

And then there was her father. He was always working–whether at his job or in church. Though the "Great Samaritans," as they were known, believed in keeping the Sabbath holy by cultivating rest, joy, and a spiritual focus, Anika couldn't understand where her father found time to sleep. He'd come home late on Saturday nights, exhausted after spending hours at church. *How could someone so committed to the church's needs find time for self-care and rest when his life seemed so consumed by his work and ministry?* This was a question Anika often pondered.

Observing her family, Anika felt that the "8 Laws of Health" didn't apply in their home. The lack of balance and the absence of proper rest made her question the validity of these teachings, especially since they didn't seem to align with her family's reality.

Yet despite her parents' shortcomings, Anika still had pleasant memories of her community. Her younger siblings, a twelve-year-old brother, and an eight-year-old sister, were devoted attendees. They often spent time playing video games quietly at the back of the room during services (thinking no one noticed). Every Saturday, they looked forward to the homemade meals the church mothers brought for everyone to enjoy after service.

With his calm and welcoming demeanor, the pastor always greeted the congregation with a smile. "Good morning and Happy Resting!" he'd say, and the congregation would smile and respond in kind. The atmosphere was always peaceful, filled with a sense of joy and serenity. The pastor often reminded everyone to leave their worries at the door, as the church was a place for peace and renewal.

Anika never missed a church service, especially when her parents were there. She was deeply involved in church activities, singing in the choir and even performing at different churches. She was an active member of the youth group, where they often chose topics or events to focus on. After the regular Saturday service, the youth group would gather later on for their evening service, continuing to connect and grow together in faith.

Often during the week, Anita's mother would invite people over, and the house would fill with laughter and chatter as family members reunited for lunch. It was a joyful occasion and a much-needed break from the stress of the day to day life. Everyone set aside their work and any lingering conflict, enjoying each other's company around the dinner table.

Anika, however, often found herself remaining quiet. For some reason, she felt disconnected from the lively conversations. The jokes her family shared seemed stale, and their discussions didn't engage her. Still, she smiled and laughed, pretending to enjoy herself, not wanting to seem rude in front of her parents. Her family often boasted about how intelligent and passionate Anika was, but inside, she felt the weight of this image. Anika didn't want to disappoint them or fall short of their expectations; sometimes the pressure was too much to bear.

Growing Older

Eventually, Anika began dating. At eighteen, she met her first boyfriend, Rob, at church. He was handsome, charismatic, and seemed to draw attention wherever he went effortlessly. Anika quickly noticed the subtle envy from other young women: the forced smiles, the sideways glances, and the whispered conversations behind her back. She knew they were jealous of their relationship for many reasons.

Rob was the leader of the youth department and was naturally charming (especially with women). He knew exactly how to win people over–guiding older women to their seats with a gentle touch and a warm smile, knowing just what to say to make someone feel special. Always dressed impeccably, Rob's dimples deepened whenever he flashed a grin, making it easy to see why so many admired him.

Likewise, Rob's admiration extended beyond the congregation. The pastor, who happened to be Rob's father, often beamed with pride. "One day, you'll take my place as pastor," he would say with confidence. In response, Rob would smile and say, "Oh, I can't wait."

At first, Anika's relationship with Rob was passive. Like others, she had admired him from afar. When he showed interest in her, she agreed to date him and developed feelings for him over time. However, something about him began to unsettle her.

One day, when Anika overheard Rob discussing the concept of submission, the way he described it made her uncomfortable. He said, "A wife has to submit to her husband, *no matter what!*" The words lingered in Anika's mind for quite some time. Rob seemed confident he could have things *his way* without question. Anika didn't want to be the type of woman who did everything her husband told her to do. *What if it led to her unhappiness? What if she felt trapped, constantly subordinating her own needs and desires to his?* These questions were a lot to consider.

Sadly, some women in their church seemed to believe that submission meant doing everything their husbands asked of them, regardless of their own feelings. Yet, Anika desired additional wisdom and understanding. *Would Rob ever care about her thoughts and feelings? Would he ever seek balance in their relationship, or was she destined to be silenced in the name of submission?* She had to know the answers.

A bit lost, Anika prayed for change. She hoped Rob would become the kind, humble, and understanding husband she had always envisioned–someone who would listen, appreciate, and respect her. However, Rob seemed to lack these qualities, leaving Anika feeling uncertain.

At times, they discussed marriage. Anika was intrigued by the idea, envisioning herself as a loving and understanding wife, eager to maintain peace and harmony. Yet, the concept of submission still felt confusing and frightening. *Was Rob right? Or was she overthinking it?* Overwhelmed, Anika began to seek advice from friends. Though few, her friends mostly shared Rob's views, repeating the same line: "A woman has to submit to her man. It's just the way it is."

Anika's heart was torn as she grappled with her own thoughts and the expectations of those around her. She didn't know where to turn or who to trust–least of all herself. The uncertainty only increased Anika's confusion about whether Rob was right in his argument. She often found herself questioning the term "submission." *What does it really mean?* To find clarity, she turned to research. She began searching through the internet and the Bible, trying to understand the true meaning behind the concept.

Unanswered Questions

In addition to her studies, Anika found herself increasingly curious about the deeper meaning of womanhood. Her questions grew more personal and required urgent answers. During a youth service at her church that week, the young people gathered in a quiet room for Bible study. The atmosphere was casual yet expectant, a space meant for discussion and spiritual growth. Anika hoped this would be the moment she could begin to explore some of the thoughts and questions that had been stirring within her. She went in eagerly.

Anika had topics of her own she wanted to discuss and anticipated straightforward answers. She had always been curious about the real-world issues that often went unspoken in church–things beyond the usual Bible stories and the simple lessons of right and wrong. Anika wanted to learn more about topics like hygiene, particularly menstruation.

For example, there was a moment in high school when Anika's math teacher, Mrs. Gravel, noticed she was holding her stomach in discomfort. "¿Estás en tu periodo?" Mrs. Gravel asked. Confused, Anika replied, "Yes, I have all my class materials!" Mrs. Gravel laughed, and Anika stared at her in confusion. The teacher leaned closer and whispered, "Honey, I asked if you were on your *period?*" It was the first time Anika had ever heard menstruation discussed in public. She couldn't help but feel a tinge of embarrassment.

The encounter stuck with Anika, and she continued to wonder why some subjects were never discussed openly at church. She wanted to talk about more than just hygiene; she was interested in cooking, ethics, culture, and sex. She also developed a growing desire to learn about managing her finances. *Why weren't these topics talked about in church?* When Anika brought this up with Rob, suggesting they address these issues in their youth group, his response was dismissive. "We can't talk about that here," he said. "There are kids around, and some people might be offended." She couldn't help but disagree with his perspective.

When she suggested talking about finances, he would say, "We don't worship money here," or "People will think we're obsessed with it." These kinds of excuses from Rob disturbed her. Why was the church so focused on staying within its four walls, discussing only religious matters?

Anika wondered how things worked in the world, especially in areas that weren't so easily explained. Adam *went* to Eve, and *suddenly*, Cain came into existence. Then, Adam *went* to Eve again, and BOOM! Abel existed. *How did that process happen exactly? Would it be inappropriate to ask? Was it a seed planted in the woman's belly that caused her to become pregnant?* Anika had many questions and very few answers.

Navigating the Chaos

Left with many unanswered questions at church, Anika began to seek counsel elsewhere. Rachel, Anika's neighbor and friend, had been by her side since childhood. After school, they would often visit each other's homes to do homework and play, their bond growing stronger over the years. Anika had confided in Rachel many times, especially about her growing frustrations and the judgmental mindset she often encountered at church. Lately, the church no longer felt like a safe or welcoming space for her–and Rachel understood.

When Anika explained how Rob spoke with such self-righteous conviction during his conversation with her, it struck a nerve in Rachel. A wave of frustration surged through her.

"See, this is *exactly* why I don't go to church," she said one day, her voice tight with emotion. "People there never think outside the box. It's like they're afraid to question anything–even when the questions are real and necessary. They're so focused on doing what they think is 'good,' but most religious people are just afraid. They avoid anything that challenges their routine or makes them uncomfortable. What's wrong with talking about real issues? Why can't we have open discussions about finances? Or about what it really means when we say wives should submit to their husbands? What about women whose husbands are abusing them? Are they still expected to submit? Is that what God wants–someone to stay in a toxic, harmful situation to appear obedient? It's like we're all completely uneducated about it. Ugh! It's like they're trapped in their own narrow-minded thinking. Thank God you have a different mindset, Anika."

As the days passed, the girls began to spend more time together. Rachel had become the one person Anika felt she could truly confide in. She was the only one who didn't judge her, who didn't try to force her into some mold that didn't fit. Rachel was a refreshing change from the rigid, often suffocating attitudes at church, and Anika needed her more than ever.

* * *

One Saturday, after church, Anika's mom prepared lunch for the entire family, a monthly tradition she hosted at home. That day, Anika invited Rachel to join them. However, things took a turn for the worse when Anika's aunt made a hurtful comment about Rachel's outfit. "Who does she think she is, showing up here dressed *like that*?" her aunt scoffed. "Is she *trying* to get a man's attention?" Rachel overheard the hurtful comment and, visibly upset, excused herself before leaving the house. She promised herself that would be the last time she ever attended one of Anika's family lunches on a Sabbath. The religious judgment was too much to bear.

At that moment, a surge of anger rose in Anika's chest. She had always viewed the Sabbath as a sacred day—one meant for peace, reflection, and freedom from judgment. But her aunt's cutting words felt like a betrayal, twisting that sacred space into something bitter and confusing. The people around her –family, church members, even friends–seemed more complicated than ever, full of hidden motives and insincere kindness. The fake smiles and practiced politeness couldn't last forever. Anika was sure of that. Eventually, the masks would fall, and when they did, she would be ready to face the truth, no matter how uncomfortable it might be.

Increasing Frustration

The following Saturday, Anika returned home from church, her heart heavy and her thoughts churning. The youth group was hosting an evening service, but she had already made up her mind–she wasn't going. She felt emotionally spent, drained by the weight of unspoken expectations and unacknowledged pain. The thought of forcing a smile and pretending everything was okay in front of people who didn't really understand her truth was unbearable. For now, she needed space–to breathe, to feel, and to begin sorting through the storm within.

The topics they discussed bored her endlessly. Every Saturday after regular service, the same predictable routine followed: "Let's meet tonight at seven to discuss a topic," the youth group would announce. It wasn't the gathering that bothered her–she enjoyed spending time with others– it was the stagnant discussions. They always revolved around food or familiar Bible stories. While these were good subjects, Anika longed for something more relevant to the world around them.

"Why don't they ever talk about what's happening in the news?" she often wondered. Anika knew the world was full of problems–political

turmoil, kidnappings, homicides, highway accidents–but it seemed like no one at church wanted to acknowledge them. What frustrated her most was the church's outright refusal to address the topic of sex. It was a subject that touched every human being, yet it was treated as taboo.

Anika firmly believed that humans were sexual beings and that this was something people needed to understand. But her parents avoided the subject entirely, as did most parents at her church. Even her pastor seemed unwilling to broach it, as though it was forbidden. This silence irritated Anika intensely. She had so many questions about what it meant to live sexually–questions no one seemed willing to answer.

Frustrated and fed up with being ignored, Anika decided to take matters into her own hands. So, she invited Rachel over to her house and decided they would learn on their own terms. They went upstairs, locked the door to her bedroom, and looked up porn on the internet. Anika wanted to see what sex *actually* looked like. While watching, she often found herself laughing at the awkward scenes, but at the same time, they satisfied her curiosity.

From there, Anika and Rachel watched movies that featured nudity and sex, trying to piece together what intimacy looked like–how people made out, touched each other, performed oral sex, and engaged in other sexual acts. For Anika, it wasn't about rebellion but about understanding.

After spending a great deal of time with Rachel, Anika felt a shift within herself. The frustration hadn't vanished, but it had softened–tempered by the comfort of being heard and understood. With a clearer mind and a steadier heart, she decided she would attend the youth service that evening after all. Maybe she wasn't ready to embrace everything the church stood for, but she wasn't prepared to walk away either. Not yet.

Much to her surprise, when she arrived, she learned that Rob had finally decided to address the topic of sex. She was thrilled. *Finally,* a subject she found relevant and meaningful! Maybe this time, it wouldn't be framed overly religiously. Anika was prepared. She sat quietly with pen and paper, ready to jot down notes. Around her, some young men seemed excited, while a few women looked curious.

Then, Rob stood up and began his presentation. "Happy Sabbath, everyone! Today, we're diving into a topic we've never discussed before. It's about...sex." He paused, smirking. "Who here has ever had sex? Raise your hand–no, I'm just kidding. Don't raise your hands," he chuckled.

The room filled with awkward laughter as Rob continued. "Sex is a gift from God. Can we all agree on that? God saw that it wasn't good for man to be alone. So, He put Adam to sleep, took one of his ribs, and created a woman–a 'womb-man,' as some say. These two were made to become one flesh. When the Bible talks about becoming one flesh, it's referring to sexual relations–a sacred act of unity. But this gift was meant for after marriage."

"Why *after* marriage?" Anika interrupted, her voice steady.

Rob's demeanor shifted. He frowned slightly and replied, "Because that's what the Bible says! No sex before marriage. No further discussion."

Anika wasn't satisfied and continued, "But there must be a reason why God forbids sex before marriage, right?"

Rob hesitated, clearly unprepared for the question. "Because...**that's what the Bible says**," he repeated, his tone defensive.

The silence in the room was heavy. Finally, an older woman chimed in, "Let's just move on, Rob. How about we talk about God's love for His children instead?"

Rob nodded in agreement.

Realizing she was not going to get the answers she was looking for, Anika sighed, frustrated and disappointed. Excusing herself, she left the group and walked towards home. Rob's gaze followed her as she exited.

* * *

When Anika arrived home earlier than usual, her mother noticed immediately. "Oh, you're back already? Did youth service finish early?" she questioned.

"No, I left," Anika replied curtly.

"What happened?" Anika hesitated, unsure how much to share. Finally, she said, "I was hoping to learn something important tonight–about sex. But I didn't learn anything new. It was the same old shallow answer."

Her mother nodded thoughtfully. "Oh, I see."

"Mom?" Anika asked tentatively. "What can *you* teach me about sex?"

Her mother chuckled nervously. "Well, it's been years since your father and I...well, *you know*. I almost forgot what it's like! Why don't you ask Rob? He seems to think he knows everything."

"Rob doesn't know *anything*," Anika muttered as she headed upstairs.

Stunned by the blunt comment, her mother stared after her, but Anika didn't care. She closed her bedroom door, grabbed her laptop, and opened it. Just as she began to distract herself, her phone rang.

"Hello?" she answered.

"Anika," Rob's voice came through, tense and accusatory. "What was *that* about? You just walked out in front of everyone."

"You were rude to me, Rob," she shot back. "I didn't appreciate it."

"Well, you didn't have to interrupt me like that. I didn't like it."

"Sorry, but if you're going to teach a topic, you need to *prepare* better."

"I'd appreciate it if you didn't ask tricky questions in front of everyone. It made me look stupid."

"You're not stupid, Rob. I'm just saying that you need to do more research on touchy subjects."

"Is *this* how you talk to your future husband, Anika!?"

She paused, her patience snapping. "Listen, I'm being real with you. You could at least listen to my advice."

Rob laughed mockingly before abruptly hanging up on her. Anika stared at her phone, furious. That was the last straw. She was done with his arrogance. The idea of submitting to him as a husband now felt laughable. As she fumed, there was a knock on her door. It opened to reveal Rachel.

"Hey!" Rachel greeted.

"Hey," Anika replied, her voice still tense.

"What's up? You look upset."

"Rob..." Anika declared angrily.

Rachel rolled her eyes. "*Ugh*, that guy. I can't stand him. So full of himself."

"And he wants to marry *me*!? **No way**."

"I'd still attend your wedding," Rachel teased, "but I wouldn't support *him*."

"There's no wedding," Anika declared firmly.

She opened her laptop and clicked on a romantic movie. Rachel joined her on the bed, and they spent the evening watching together, letting the tension melt away. As Rachel and Anika watched the film, Anika's thoughts kept drifting. She was captivated by a scene of a couple making out in bed, and it sparked questions within her. *What would it feel like to love someone truly? To make love with someone she cared about? To hold someone close and be held in return?* These were experiences she had never shared with Rob.

Their six-month relationship had been devoid of physical intimacy. Rob was adamant about not touching a woman before marriage, a decision Anika assumed stemmed from his desire to honor their families' expectations. While she respected his choice, she couldn't help but feel the distance it created. What troubled her more was their complete avoidance of discussing sex, whether in marriage or in general. Abstinence, she thought, didn't mean silence. *It should be okay to talk about these things, shouldn't it?*

As the movie played on, Anika felt her body stirring with unfamiliar emotions. A longing was building within her–a desire to understand and experience the intimacy she saw on screen. She imagined what it might be like to have a man next to her, feel his touch, and share something deeply personal and physical. But these thoughts remained locked away, unspoken and private.

* * *

Two hours later, the movie ended, and Rachel had fallen asleep on Anika's bed. Anika smiled as she glanced at her friend, now snoring softly. Rachel had been her closest companion for years, almost like a sister. Growing up, Rachel had always taken the lead, playing "mommy" during their Barbie games and ensuring they cleaned up before their parents returned home.

Now, watching her childhood friend sleep peacefully, Anika felt a wave of nostalgia wash over her. She let Rachel rest undisturbed while she grabbed her sketchbook and crayons. Sitting at her desk, she began to draw, letting her mind wander. She started with trees, rivers, and flowers, her usual comfort zone. The bright colors brought her sketches to life, and the act of drawing calmed her restless thoughts.

As her hand moved across the page, Anika's focus shifted. Without consciously deciding to, Anika found herself drawing a man and a woman. The man stood behind the woman, kissing her neck tenderly, his hand sliding under the waistband of her underwear. The woman's eyes were closed, her expression one of pleasure and trust.

Anika continued to sketch, adding details that brought the scene to life. She didn't shy away from intimacy in her art. She drew men's bodies, exposed and raw, and allowed her imagination to guide her pencil. Her drawings became her secret diary, a place where she could express feelings she couldn't put into words. Each stroke of the crayon freed her thoughts, capturing the emotions she kept locked away. She had no shame in what she drew—this was her outlet, her way of understanding herself. For Anika, her art was more than just pictures; it was her voice and way of exploring desires and questions that no one seemed willing to discuss.

Education is Key

The following week, the youth gathered for a special Wednesday evening Bible study at church. Participation was encouraged, and everyone was asked to come prepared with questions to spark meaningful discussion. Anika decided to give the youth group one last chance. With thoughtful intention, she jotted down a few questions before heading to church. As she stepped into the room, she noticed Rob and a few others already seated. At the front, the presenter, William, stood ready to guide the evening's conversation.

"Tonight," William began, "we'll be talking about the temple of God." Anika leaned forward slightly, intrigued.

"Well, that's *interesting,*" she thought.

William continued, "We're surrounded by sexual imagery everywhere. Ads for women's lingerie are plastered on billboards and buses. In Hollywood movies, nudity and sex are almost expected. And then there's the issue of how some women dress in public. I have sons at home, and shielding them from what they see is a struggle. Even at home, commercials feature women with large breasts walking around in nothing but a bra and underwear. It's hard to avoid."

Anika raised her hand. "Do you think it's important to teach children about these things early on?"

"Absolutely," William replied. "Education is key. We should be proactive, researching what's happening in the world. Kids, teens, and young adults need to know about life outside the church walls."

"That's *right*," Anika agreed.

Rob glanced at her, his expression unreadable. She couldn't tell if he thought she was being genuine or mocking him.

"Well," Rob began, his tone measured but pointed, "back to the temple topic. I believe we're responsible for what we expose ourselves to. It's a shame to watch movies filled with impurity, like people having sex before marriage or cursing. Let's be honest: those things go against our values. Don't you agree, *Anika*?"

Anika's stomach tightened. She thought to herself, "*What the heck is his problem? Why is he singling me out?*"

Rob continued, addressing the group but clearly targeting her. "It's a struggle, sure. But we know better. We should avoid anything that disturbs our spirit. I know for a fact that my fiancée watches Hollywood movies. Some other people here probably do too."

Anika felt her blood boil. She couldn't believe his audacity. "Well," she said, her voice sharp, "what about you, Mr. 'I-never-watched-porn-ever-in-my-life'!? What do *you* know about purity? Care to enlighten us?"

The room fell silent. William quickly said, "Anika, it's inappropriate to talk to your fiancé like that."

"He's **not** my fiancé," Anika shot back. "And he has no right to humiliate me in front of everyone."

With that, she stood up and walked out–again. Anika left the church building without a second thought, unconcerned about how her abrupt exit might be perceived. She was done–*done* with Rob and his condescension. His attitude had crossed the line one too many times, and she couldn't tolerate it anymore. Perhaps she had once been the shy girl who quietly endured his remarks, but she wasn't that girl anymore. At least she didn't *want* to be that girl anymore. If Rob wanted a woman who nodded along and said "Amen" to his every word, *that* woman wouldn't be Anika.

For the first time since she met him, she questioned why the girls at church adored him so much. Some of them would have given anything to be in her position. "*They can have him for all I care,*" she thought bitterly. His lousy attitude had soured any affection she might have had for him.

When Anika got home, she went straight to her room and shut the door behind her. She picked up her sketchbook and started drawing a furious woman. The woman's face brimmed with rage, her eyes wild, her fists clenched. Anika poured her emotions onto the page. The woman in her drawing wasn't just angry–she was disillusioned. She believed in a love story, only to discover that the man she thought was perfect was a fraud. A mask hid his arrogance, his flaws, and his insincerity.

Anika began to question herself. *Had she ignored the red flags? His need to show off, his flirtations with other women at church, and his overconfidence–were they all signs that he wasn't the one for her!?* She had convinced herself that he might change someday, that there was hope for his heart. *But wasn't that just wishful thinking? Wasn't she wasting her time?*

Then there were her parents. They spent so much time at church that Anika often felt like an afterthought. Her father was a workaholic, dividing his energy between his job and church duties, leaving him with little time for his family. Meanwhile, her mother was always busy organizing church activities and baking cookies for the youth group. Anika was left at home to care for her siblings, spending little to no meaningful time with her parents. She felt like she wasn't receiving the support she desperately needed.

Their lack of closeness hurt her. They never talked about love, relationships, sex, or marriage. Her parents seemed to live together out of habit, not passion. There was no visible spark, no warmth between them, and it deeply disturbed Anika. *"What does true love look like?"* she wondered.

* * *

Feeling overwhelmed, Anika needed an escape. In desperation, she turned back to pornography. It became her way of exploring the questions and desires she felt no one else was willing to address.

Anika watched scene after scene, feeding her imagination with the sexual scenarios. She didn't care if it was taboo. She loved the confidence the women exuded, their ease with their partners, and their apparent mastery of intimacy.

Yet, as she watched, she began to compare herself to them. She scrutinized her own body and personality against theirs. They seemed so poised and alluring. Anika, by contrast, felt inadequate–unattractive, inexperienced, and unsure of herself. She began to resent the restrictions placed on her by her upbringing. She wanted to explore life beyond the rigid boundaries of church and religion.

As she continued to watch, her anger deepened. She was furious that her parents had never talked to her about sex. She resented the church for avoiding the topic entirely and judging her whenever she asked "weird" questions. *Was it so wrong to be curious? Was it abnormal to have these feelings?* When her frustrations had finally boiled over, she made a decision: she was **done** with church. From that point on, she stopped attending weekly Bible studies and began to distance herself from her religious community. Anika wanted to break free. She craved a deeper understanding of the world outside her sheltered life.

A Special Guest

At school, Anita carried on as usual. She looked forward to her Thursday afternoon class, "Individual and Society." It was one of her favorite courses–a space for openly discussing real-world issues.

One particular day, the class had a special guest: Marie, a former prostitute. Marie's story captivated Anika. Marie had left her past behind and built a new life. She had gotten married, had two children, and had dreams of opening an orphanage. Marie believed every child deserved to grow up in a home filled with love and respect. Her message was one of purpose, resilience, and compassion.

Listening to Marie, Anika felt a spark of hope. Here was a woman who had overcome judgment and hardship to create something beautiful. Marie's words stirred something deep inside Anika–a desire to find her own purpose and build a life rooted in authenticity and self-discovery.

The more Anika listened to Marie, the more she learned. As a child, Marie had endured abuse at the hands of her own father. Whenever they were alone at home, she lived in constant fear of him. By the time she turned thirteen, she couldn't take it anymore and ran away to escape the nightmare.

One evening, she and a couple of her girlfriends decided to go to a nightclub. Desperate to blend into an adult world that felt far removed from her pain, they deceptively secured fake IDs, allowing them entry. That night, she met a man who immediately caught her attention. He was known as "Mr. Snake," a nickname earned from the vivid red serpent tattoo that slithered up the left side of his neck–impossible to miss and hard to forget.

To Marie's young eyes, Mr. Snake seemed impossibly handsome. And it didn't take long before he noticed her as well. From across the dance floor, his gaze lingered on Marie, filled with interest. She felt seen in a way she hadn't before, and when Mr. Snake finally approached her, she was both nervous and flattered. They danced together under the pulsing lights, her friends watching approvingly from a distance.

Later that night, Marie and Mr. Snake moved to a quieter corner and struck up a conversation. Mr. Snake was charming, and his attention made her feel special, even safe for a fleeting moment. By the end of the night, they had exchanged phone numbers. She thought she had found someone who could take her away from her troubles.

After that, Marie stayed over at a girlfriend's house. She didn't want to return to her parents' home because of her father. While at her friend's house, she spent most of the night texting Mr. Snake. Their conversation quickly became flirtatious, with both exchanging sexual comments. She thought her actions were nothing more than harmless joking, but she would eventually learn otherwise.

A few days later, Marie and Mr. Snake met at a bar, where they drank together. From that point on, her memory was a haze. She couldn't recall how she ended up at his apartment–only that she was drunk and drugged.

Mr. Snake had betrayed her by selling her to a drug dealer. Together, Marie traveled with the man to another city, where she was forced into stripping and coerced into prostitution to earn money. She was just thirteen years old.

"That's illegal," one student interrupted.

"Yes, it is," Marie replied solemnly. "And sadly, it's still happening today."

"What happened to Mr. Snake?" another student asked.

"Well," Marie sighed, "the police haven't caught him yet."

"Students, let her finish her story. You can ask questions later," the teacher interjected gently.

Marie continued, "All I'm saying is that sometimes in life, you'll encounter people who care only about your *body*, not your mind. They don't see you for who you are–they only want to use you. I don't know what you all may be searching for in life, but whatever it is, you won't find it in those dark places. Prostitution is not the answer if you're hoping for a better life. It's like slavery–you're controlled by pimps who force you to do whatever they want. If you refuse, they'll beat you. In the end, you're being paid to endure abuse and be violated. It's no way to live. And prostitution doesn't just involve physical harm–it takes a devastating toll on your emotional and mental health. Many experience severe trauma, a deep sense of emptiness, poor nutrition, and a significant decline in self-esteem. Drugs and alcohol are often introduced as part of this life, creating an even darker spiral. As a result, many women struggle with suicidal thoughts, and tragically, some lose their lives–either at the hands of clients or pimps. It's a cycle of exploitation and destruction that leaves lasting scars."

Marie's final words laid a heavy glaze of silence over the classroom. Taking a moment to let it all sink in, she eventually glanced at the teacher, signaling that she had finished speaking. Then the classroom erupted with applause. Everyone was touched by Marie's story.

When the applause finally died down, the teacher stood and addressed the class, "If you have any questions, please form a line. Marie will be happy to answer them, but I ask that you keep your responses brief—no more than three minutes each—as I have another class starting soon. Thank you."

With that, Anika quickly made her way to the front of the line. "Hi, I'm Anika," she said with a warm smile. "I have a question. Was it difficult to get married and have kids after everything you've been through? How did you do it?"

Marie smiled softly. "Well...that's a long story. I host a free workshop on the first Saturday of every month on Beverly Street. We cover a wide range of topics, and you're welcome to ask me anything you'd like. You're also welcome to email me anytime—it would be a pleasure to discuss this with you, Anika."

"Thank you," Anika replied, noting Marie's email before leaving the classroom with a grateful smile. "I sure will."

CHAPTER 2

The Spark of Revolution, the Fury of Rebellion

After a while, Anika considered moving out of her family home to rent an apartment. She longed for independence–the freedom to live without anyone dictating her choices. She wanted a space to call her own. Now, she sat in front of her computer screen, engrossed in job applications. A full-time job was her goal, something that would provide financial stability and allow her to cover her bills independently.

As she typed away and focused on her task, there was a knock at her bedroom door. It was her mother.

"Anika, aren't you coming to church? We're ready!" her mother called out.

"I'm not coming, Mom. I'm busy," Anika replied, her eyes still glued to the screen.

"Busy with what? You've been at that computer for almost three weeks now," her mother said, stepping into the room.

"I'm looking for jobs online," Anika explained.

"Sweetheart, you need to rest. It's the Sabbath. You can do this later tonight," her mother said gently.

"I don't want to, Mom," Anika insisted. "I need a job as soon as possible."

Anika heard her mother's footsteps fading as she walked away. Turning back to her computer, she resumed her job search. After scrolling, a listing caught her eye: **"Secretary wanted for a full-time position."**

She clicked on the link and carefully read through the job description. It seemed like the perfect opportunity. Hopeful, she quickly submitted her résumé online and added the company to her growing list of applications. Previously, she had applied to various positions, including call centers, boutiques, and other businesses. Now, all she could do was wait for a phone call or email response.

* * *

Two hours later, Anika's inbox pinged with a new email. It was from a hotel called *Waterfalls*, where she had applied a week ago for a front desk representative role. The position was full-time–just what she needed. Excited yet nervous, Anika opened the email and began reading: **"Please call for an interview over the phone. You can contact Mrs. Damien at 555-8237. Thank you. We look forward to hearing from you**."

Anika stared at the email, her heart racing with cautious optimism. *Could this finally be it?* Without hesitation, she picked up her phone and dialed the number. **Yes**, she made the call on a Sabbath day–a *day* meant for rest and reflection. The *day* she was supposed to be at church, not sitting in front of her computer. The *day* when whispers from envious women at church about her and Rob shouldn't echo in her mind. The day when no cutting remarks should be made over a dinner table. After all, *wasn't the Sabbath meant to be a holy day filled with peace, smiles, and joy?*

Well, enough was enough. Anika had stopped caring. She was done with the rules, the expectations, and the judgment. She was tired of living in a box built by others. With a steady hand and newfound resolve, Anika dialed the number. She wasn't going to let anything hold her back–not *today*.

The phone rang, and the interview began immediately. The interviewer asked Anika a series of questions, and at first, everything seemed to go well. But then, the catch came. Anika was told she needed at least three years of experience in the field–experience she didn't have.

"I'm eager to learn more about this role," Anika offered, hoping her enthusiasm would compensate for her lack of qualifications. But the interviewer wasn't swayed. Her proposition was politely declined, and the call ended abruptly.

Disheartened, Anika set her phone down and stared blankly at the screen. Frustration bubbled up, and she dialed her friend Rachel.

"Rachel, I can't take this anymore," Anika said, her voice tinged with exhaustion. "It's been three weeks of applying and getting rejection after rejection. Every email says I'm unsuitable for this or that position. And *today*? I finally got an interview, but I couldn't even land the job because I wasn't qualified. I'm so tired of this crap!"

"Anika, you've got to be patient," Rachel said gently. "Some people search for months before they find something–sometimes even a year. Don't give up just yet."

"*A year?*" Anika groaned. "You really expect me to wait that long?"

Rachel laughed lightly. "I know it sucks, but you've got to keep going. Tell you what—there's a party tonight. I was invited, and maybe it'll take your mind off things. Want to come with me? Unless, of course, your parents won't let you. You know how they are about partying…"

"Shut up, Rachel," Anika shot back with a faint smile. "I'll come with you."

"Great! Some friends of mine will pick us up. I'll text you the details!" Rachel chirped.

Anika sighed. A night out was exactly what she needed. "Alright. See you tonight," Anika said as she hung up the phone. She got up from her bed and walked over to her wardrobe, rummaging through her clothes to find the perfect outfit for the evening.

While she was sorting through her options, she heard the sound of keys jingling downstairs. Her parents were home from church.

"Anika!" her mom called out. "People were asking about you—they said hi!"

"Okay, thanks!" Anika shouted back, trying to keep her tone casual.

"And Rob says hi too! He mentioned he's been calling and texting you all morning."

Anika froze for a moment but chose not to respond. She knew Rob had been trying to reach her—she'd seen the missed calls and unread messages. But she'd deliberately put her phone on silent to avoid dealing with him. Shaking off the thought, she focused on the clothes before her.

After a few minutes of deliberation, she selected one of her best outfits for the night. Feeling confident, she texted Rachel quickly: **"Let's go! I'm ready!"**

Heading downstairs, Anika called out, "Mom, Dad, I'm going out with Rachel! I'll see you later!"

"Alright, be careful!" her mom replied. "And tell Rachel I said hi!"

Her mother didn't worry much about Anika hanging out with Rachel. The two had been inseparable since childhood, and their families had been friends for years–Rachel's and Anika's parents had even gone to high school together. With that reassurance in mind, Anika stepped out, ready to leave behind the stress of the past few weeks, if only for one night.

* * *

When Anika and Rachel arrived at the house party, the atmosphere hit them immediately–loud music pumped through the speakers and the DJ was expertly mixing beats that kept the crowd energized. The dance area was packed, with people moving to the rhythm while others sat around tables playing cards and chatting. Anika stuck close to Rachel, feeling out of place in a room full of strangers. No one from her church crowd would ever attend a party like this.

As they made their way toward the living room, they passed a table lined with an assortment of alcoholic drinks. Rachel grabbed a cup for herself and handed one to Anika.

"Here," Rachel said, grinning. "Don't worry, I won't let you get drunk. I'm keeping an eye on you."

Anika hesitated momentarily before taking a small sip–it was the first time she'd ever held a drink, let alone tasted alcohol.

Rachel's eyes lit up mischievously as they stood chatting by the wall. "Ohhhh, Anikaaaa. It looks like someone here has an eye on you," she teased, nudging her friend.

"Stop it!" Anika replied, her cheeks flushing as she glanced at Rachel.

But her curiosity got the better of her. Turning slightly, she caught sight of a man watching her from across the room. He was standing with a group of friends, but his focus was clearly on her. Embarrassed, she quickly looked away and faced Rachel again, pretending not to notice.

"Oh my gosh," Rachel said, barely containing her excitement. "He's coming. He's coming towards *you*!"

Anika felt her heart race as Rachel's words proved true. She felt a tap on her shoulder and turned around.

"Hi," he said, his voice warm but slightly hesitant.

"Hi," Anika replied, her tone cautious yet polite.

"I'm Boris," he introduced himself, extending his hand.

At twenty-five, Boris was a college student who exuded effortless charm. His confident smile and charismatic presence made him stand out in any crowd, drawing people in with his natural ease and magnetic personality. Whether in class or at social gatherings, Boris had a way of captivating those around him.

"Nice to meet you, Boris. I'm Anika," she said, shaking his hand.

He slid his hands into his pockets, and Anika noticed he seemed a little nervous.

"First time I've seen you here," he said, breaking the silence.

"Yeah, it's my first time," she replied. "I came with my friend Ra–"

Anika glanced around, thinking Rachel was still beside her, but her friend had wandered off to chat with other people, leaving her alone with Boris.

"Looks like your friend ditched you," Boris said with a small laugh. "Don't worry, though. This place is safe, and honestly, it's a great spot to meet people. Partying's a nice break after long days of school or work."

"Yeah, I guess so," Anika replied, offering a polite smile.

"So, where do you work? If you don't mind me asking," he continued, his tone casual.

"I'm unemployed at the moment," Anika admitted. "But I'm actively looking for a job."

"Right," Boris said, nodding knowingly. "It's tough finding a good job these days."

"Tell me about it," Anika said, her voice tinged with frustration.

"I work as an engineer, full-time," he shared. "It's a bit of a commute, but it pays well, so I can't complain."

"That's great," she said genuinely.

"Yeah. So, do you live on your own or with your family?"

"I live with my parents," Anika replied, feeling self-conscious.

"Ah, I see," Boris said with understanding.

"Hopefully not for much longer," Anika added quickly. "Once I find a well-paying job, I plan to move out and get my own place."

"That's a good plan," he said with a nod. "Having your independence is important."

There was a brief pause before Boris smiled. "Hey, would you mind exchanging numbers? I want to keep in touch if that's okay with you?"

"Sure," Anika said, reciting her number. "555-2938."

"Got it. I'll text you so you'll have my number, too," Boris said with a smile.

"Alright," Anika said, feeling curious and nervous.

After exchanging numbers, their conversation deepened. They discussed their aspirations and favorite hobbies, sharing a few laughs along the way. Across the room, Rachel caught sight of them and gave Anika a playful wink, clearly amused by the scene.

Hours passed, and the party began winding down. Guests started to leave, and Rachel signaled to Anika that it was time to head out.

"It was nice chatting with you, Boris. Hope to see you again soon," Anika said, feeling excitement and nervousness.

"We definitely will," Boris replied with a confident smile. "Have a good night."

As Anika walked toward the car with Rachel, she couldn't help but reflect on the evening. She'd come to the party hoping to relax and have a good time, but she hadn't expected to meet someone like Boris.

Once they got into the car, Rachel wasted no time. "Soooooo, how was your convo with that guy?" she teased, glancing at Anika with a mischievous grin.

"It went well," Anika said, smiling. "We talked about school, and I told him about my dream of becoming an entrepreneur someday. He seemed genuinely interested in getting to know me more. He even mentioned wanting to take me out for coffee this week."

"That's awesome!" Rachel said, clearly excited. "But just be careful with guys like him. Don't fall too quickly! He might seem nice now, but you never know. He could turn out to be another Rob. Haha!"

Anika chuckled lightly, but a pang of uncertainty still lingered. She hoped Boris wouldn't be another Rob. At least he had a stable career and seemed driven. She was cautiously optimistic, looking forward to where this connection might lead.

Something New

Over time, Boris and Anika started officially dating. They had quickly fallen into a rhythm, speaking on the phone almost every day, their conversations brimming with shared dreams and laughter. On weekends, they would hang out at the library, and on evenings, they would indulge in movies or dine at cozy restaurants. Boris seemed to tick every box for Anika–he was charming, intelligent, and undeniably attractive.

At night, after their long conversations, Anika often found herself lost in fantasies about him. She imagined his hands exploring her, his lips trailing soft kisses, the warmth of their bodies pressed together in a passionate embrace. These thoughts filled her mind, leaving her both excited and restless. Boris had awakened something she hadn't fully understood before–a yearning she could no longer ignore.

One evening, they sat together in a café. The warm glow of the overhead lights cast a golden hue over their table as Boris casually mentioned his roommate.

"He's heading back to India soon," Boris said. "Which means I'll have the place to myself for a while. You should come over sometime–we could chill out."

Anika froze for a moment, his suggestion stirring conflicting emotions within her. She thought back to the youth group meetings at church, where they were repeatedly warned about the dangers of being alone with a significant other in private spaces. She had always dismissed those rules as overly restrictive, but now, the cautionary words lingered in her mind.

"I don't think that's a good idea," she said finally, her voice tinged with hesitation.

Boris didn't press her. "That's fine," he said with a reassuring smile. "No pressure. Maybe some other time."

"Maybe," she replied, though uncertainty tugged at her.

After their café date, Boris drove her home. The car was quiet at first, save for the soft hum of the engine and the occasional crackle of the radio. Boris talked about his weekend plans, but Anika's focus drifted. She couldn't stop stealing glances at him–his freshly trimmed hair, the crisp lines of his dress shirt that highlighted his muscular chest, and how his hands confidently gripped the steering wheel.

Her pulse quickened. The attraction she had been holding back was overwhelming her.

"Boris?" she said, her voice almost a whisper.

He glanced at her briefly before turning his eyes back to the road. "Yeah?"

"Can you...stop the car? Maybe park somewhere private?"

He frowned slightly, a mix of curiosity and concern crossing his face. "Why? What's wrong?"

"Nothing's wrong," she said, her cheeks flushing. "I just...I want some time alone with you."

Realization dawned on his face, and without a word, he nodded. He turned off the main road onto a quiet, dimly lit side street and parked the car.

As soon as he shifted into the park, Anika leaned toward him and kissed him. It began as a soft, tentative kiss, but the intensity grew quickly. Boris responded, pulling her closer, his hands resting on her waist as she climbed onto his lap.

Their lips moved in sync, the heat between them rising. Anika ran her fingers through his hair while his arms tightened around her. It was a moment she had fantasized about for weeks, and now it was real–electric, passionate, and raw. For a while, nothing else mattered. The world outside the car disappeared, leaving only the two of them lost in their connection.

Then Boris asked, "Want to move to the back seat?"

"No," Anika replied firmly, though her voice softened. "I just want to make out with you."

They continued kissing, the intensity growing with every passing second. Anika could feel Boris's arousal as she straddled him, and for a moment, she lost her breath. The realization sent a wave of uncertainty through her. She pulled back, breaking the kiss abruptly.

"Sorry," she murmured, her cheeks flushed. "You can drop me off at home now."

Boris gave her a small, understanding smile, though there was a flicker of disappointment in his eyes. "Alright," he said.

Before sliding back into her seat, she kissed him one last time–a gentle peck, almost apologetic. As she fastened her seatbelt, her mind raced, "*Was I crazy to do this? What's he thinking about me right now? Did I seem too forward? Or maybe too hesitant?*" Anika was unsure.

The ride home was quiet. Neither of them spoke, and the silence was heavy but not uncomfortable. Boris kept his focus on the road, occasionally glancing at her as if trying to gauge her emotions. He finally broke the silence when they pulled up in front of her house.

"I'll call you later tonight," he said, his voice warm and reassuring.

Anika felt a wave of relief. He still wanted to talk to her despite her worries about how the moment in the car might have come across. That was a good sign.

"Okay," she replied, smiling faintly.

They kissed one more time before she got out of the car. As she walked up to her door, she glanced back to see him watching her. She gave him a small wave before heading inside.

Later, in her room, Anika lay on her bed, still replaying the events of the night. She couldn't shake the mix of excitement and awkwardness that lingered, "*Did I overdo it? Or maybe not do enough? What was he thinking now?*"

Her thoughts were interrupted by the buzz of her phone. It was Boris calling.

"Hello," she said, her voice steady but nervous.

"Hey, Anika," he replied. "Are you home safe?"

"Yeah, I'm home. You?"

"I'm good; I just got in. I wanted to say...I really enjoyed tonight. Spending time with you was great."

"I enjoyed it too," she said, hesitating slightly. "Even...the *car scene*?"

Boris laughed softly. "*Especially* the car scene. I've wanted to kiss you like that since our first date."

Anika felt her cheeks heat up. "Glad you enjoyed it. I just wasn't ready for anything more."

"It's okay," he said gently. "Really. I get it. It's not something to rush into."

The reassurance in his voice eased her nerves.

After a pause, she decided to leap. "Boris...have you ever thought about, um, phone sex?"

He chuckled, caught off guard. "Phone sex? With you? I didn't think you'd ever bring that up."

"What makes you say that?" she asked, a hint of defensiveness creeping into her tone.

"Well," he said carefully, "you've always seemed like the sweet, quiet type. A good girl. Not the kind of person to, *you know*."

Anika frowned slightly. She didn't want to be boxed into an image of being shy anymore. "People change," she said firmly.

Boris seemed to sense her shift in tone. "Fair enough," he said, his voice softer. "To answer your question...yeah, I've done it before."

"Would you want to have phone sex with me?"

There was a brief pause before he responded, his tone laced with a mix of curiosity and playfulness. "With you? Yeah. I'd like that. It would definitely help me sleep tonight."

Anika's heart raced. It was uncharted territory for her, but she wanted to explore it. She felt ready to try something new and push boundaries she'd never dared to approach. If this was the first step toward intimacy, she was willing to take it.

"Okay," she said softly. "Let's try."

And with that, they ventured into a thrilling and nerve-wracking moment, a new chapter in their growing connection.

"I'm not as creative as you might think," Anika admitted, her voice hesitant.

Boris chuckled softly. "It's okay. It's simpler than you think. You've seen movies with love scenes. Just let yourself be inspired. Describe what you feel or what you imagine. Trust me."

"Alright," she said, biting her lip nervously. "You start. I want to see how you do it."

"Fair enough," he said. There was a brief pause, and Anika could hear him adjusting in bed. His tone became lower, more intimate. "I love hearing your voice. It's so sexy–just listening to you gets me going."

Anika hesitated for a moment before finding her words. "I've been thinking about you all day," she said softly. "I've been imagining kissing you all night long."

"I can't stop thinking about how you climbed onto me in the car," Boris said, his voice thick with desire. "The way you moaned while we kissed, how your thighs felt under my hands, how soft your skin was. I *loved* touching you."

Her cheeks flushed as she responded, "I loved how your lips felt on my neck, how you kissed me down to my chest. It made me want you even more."

"Hmm," he murmured. "Right now, I'm slipping my hand under my pants. What about you? What are you wearing?"

Anika swallowed hard, her heart racing. "I'm wearing a pink robe," she said, trembling slightly. "I just got out of the shower."

"Damn," Boris said, his breath quickening. "You must look so hot in that robe."

"I wish you were here with me," she continued, her confidence growing. "I want to feel your arms around me again. I want you so bad."

"How bad do you want me?" he asked, his voice dripping with anticipation.

"If you were here, I'd rip your shirt off," she said, her words slow and deliberate. "I'd kiss you all over–your lips, your chest...and then I'd have you right here, right *now*."

She could hear his breathing intensify. His occasional moans told her he was completely immersed in the moment. On the other hand, Anika had decided she wouldn't touch herself. She felt uncomfortable doing it, but was committed to keeping his mood alive.

Her words seemed to do the trick. Boris's moans grew louder, and she could tell he was nearing his climax. The sound of his pleasure filled her ears, and though the experience was new and strange, she felt a thrill knowing she had this effect on him.

After about an hour, their conversation began to wind down. Anika heard Boris let out one final, satisfied sigh. "That was incredible," he said, his voice soft and tired.

"Glad you enjoyed it," Anika said, smiling to herself.

They exchanged goodnights, and Anika hung up the phone. She lay in bed, feeling a mix of emotions–excitement, curiosity, and a sense of accomplishment. The experience had been a step outside her comfort zone, but she felt closer to Boris because of it.

* * *

The next morning, Anika went downstairs for breakfast. The smell of coffee filled the air, and her mother sorted through the mail at the kitchen table.

"Good morning," her mother said, glancing up.

"Morning," Anika replied, pouring herself a cup of tea.

Her mother looked at her curiously. "You're up late today. Long night?"

Anika froze for a moment, then gave a casual shrug. "I was just on the phone."

Her mother raised an eyebrow but didn't press further. "Hmm. Well, don't let late nights ruin your mornings. You still need to keep your routine."

Anika nodded, hiding a small smile as she sipped her tea. She had no intention of revealing what her night had truly entailed.

"What is *this*?" Anika's mother asked sharply, her gaze fixed on Anika's neck.

"What is what?" Anika replied, her voice unsteady.

"That *thing*! On your neck! What is it?"

"Oh, snap," Anika thought, realizing the hickey Boris had left was still visible.

"It's just a rash," she said, hoping to deflect her mother's suspicion.

Her mother narrowed her eyes. "Just a rash, huh? Who dropped you off last night?"

"A friend."

"A *friend*..." Her mother's tone was skeptical. "I keep seeing the same black car in front of the house. Who were you with, Anika?"

"A *friend*, Mom," Anika said firmly, trying to end the conversation.

"You know Rob will not be happy to hear this," her mother said pointedly. "You two are already talking about marriage. Don't embarrass him, Anika."

"Don't embarrass *him*? What about me?" Anika snapped. "Does anyone care about how I feel? I don't want to be with Rob anymore!"

Her mother looked at her in disbelief. "You're going to leave him for some other man? Someone outside the church? But–Rob is a good Christian!"

"Rob is not the saint everyone thinks he is," Anika said, her voice trembling with frustration. "Just because he knows the Bible and can charm people doesn't make him a true Christian. He appears godly, but inside, he's carrying rotten fruit. I've seen it. I've spent enough time with him to know. I'm done pretending, Mom. Religion isn't my thing anymore. I want to be free. I want to live my own life."

"You want to *what*–ruin your life?!" her mother shouted, her voice rising. "You've always been such a well-behaved, educated child. You have a good reputation and now you want to throw it all away?"

Anika didn't respond. Her anger boiled over as she got up and stormed out of the kitchen. The judgment from her mom was too much to navigate.

Back in her room, she slammed the door shut. She felt trapped, suffocated by her parents' expectations. Anika wanted to be treated like an adult, not controlled like a child.

She grabbed her phone and called Boris. "Can you come pick me up, please? I'm at home," she said, her voice still emotionless.

"I'm on my way," Boris replied without hesitation.

* * *

It didn't take long before they arrived at Boris's apartment. Anika followed him inside, taking in the neat and cozy space. They sat on the couch together.

"I was reading this book before you called," Boris said, holding up a novel.

Anika gave a half-hearted smile as he continued reading. She stood and wandered around the apartment, inspecting the framed photos on the shelves and the minimalist décor. It was clean, orderly, and very Boris.

She returned to the couch and sat down beside him. Her hand rested lightly on his thigh, then began to trace small circles. Boris paused mid-sentence, glancing at her hand. He understood her intent and closed the book, setting it aside.

He removed his shirt and leaned in, his lips brushing against hers. They kissed deeply, their movements growing more urgent. Anika unbuckled his belt and slid his pants down, her breath quickening. At the same time, he helped her remove her clothing. Unclothed, Boris took her by the hand and led her to his bedroom.

Inside, the atmosphere shifted. The soft light from the bedside lamp bathed the room in a warm glow. Boris lay her gently on the bed, climbing on top of her. He kissed her neck, and she ran her hands over his back, her fingers tracing the muscles beneath his skin.

Boris paused to retrieve a condom from the drawer. Tearing open the wrapper, he quickly put it on and met Anika's gaze.

"Go slowly," Anika whispered, her eyes locking with his.

Boris nodded, his movements careful and deliberate. They both navigated this intimate moment with a mixture of vulnerability and desire, exploring a connection that had been building between them for weeks.

Boris slowly entered her, and she felt a sharp twinge of pain at first. He moved carefully, and she held his gaze, her eyes locked on his face.

Occasionally, he leaned down to kiss her, a gesture of tenderness amidst the intimacy. And *there* it was–this was **sex**.

After about ten minutes, he rolled off her, lying back on the bed. Anika stared at the ceiling, her mind racing. It felt surreal. She didn't know what to think of herself or what to feel. She couldn't believe what had just happened. The silence hung between them until a thought stirred within her. She didn't want this awkwardness to define her first experience. Tentatively, she reached for Boris, and they began again. Her nervousness began to melt away the second time, then the third. She let herself embrace the moment, realizing that sex could feel good–intimate and free.

All those warnings from the church about fornication–that it would lead to ruin, disease, or disgrace–flashed through her mind. But none of it happened. She wasn't dead. She wasn't consumed by guilt. Anika was alive and she felt fine. No, more than fine. She felt *great*.

Eventually, it became late, and Anika knew she had to go home. Her parents were probably worried sick. She and Boris dressed quietly, sharing a few lingering touches and smiles as they prepared to leave.

On the drive back, Boris held her hand the entire time. She couldn't stop smiling at him, a giddy warmth bubbling inside her. When they arrived in front of her house, she leaned over, kissed him softly, and whispered, "Good night."

"Good night," he replied, watching as she stepped out of the car and slipped inside.

The house was dark and silent. It seemed like everyone was asleep. Anika tiptoed across the living room, trying to avoid making a sound.

Click.

The kitchen light flickered on, and her father stood in the doorway, his expression stern.

"Miss Anika Bailes," he began, his voice low but firm. "Your mother has been worried sick. She's been calling you all night. Why didn't you answer your phone?"

"I'm sorry, Dad," Anika mumbled, her mind scrambling for an excuse. "I didn't check my phone. I was already on my way back."

"You need to call your mother when you're out late and tell her who you're with. I want the number of this 'friend' next time."

"Yes, Dad. I'll call her next time," she said, forcing herself to sound contrite, even though the promise was hollow.

He studied her for a moment, then sighed. "I'm glad you're safe. Go to bed."

Her father turned off the light and headed back to his room. Anika exhaled in relief and crept up the stairs. Once in her room, she peeled off her clothes, took a quick shower, and slipped into her pajamas.

Lying in bed, she stared at the ceiling again. Her thoughts were racing. She couldn't keep living under her parents' watchful eyes, constantly justifying herself, feeling like a child. She needed freedom and independence.

Her gaze drifted to her wardrobe, and the idea began to form: what if she packed up her things and moved in with Boris? Living with him would mean no more curfews, no more lectures, and no more guilt. It seemed like the perfect opportunity.

Her phone buzzed, pulling her out of her thoughts. It was a text from Boris:

"Good night."

She replied, "**Good night...I'm moving in with you tomorrow**."

As soon as she hit send, doubt crept in. *Was she thinking too fast? What if he said no?* She turned off her phone, frustration boiling inside her. Her parents' control had pushed her to this decision, but she also hoped this leap would be a fresh start, a new adventure. She laid down on the bed, and closed her eyes. Maybe some rest would help her process everything she was feeling.

* * *

The next morning, Anika turned her phone back on. She had missed calls and several texts from Boris. Nervously, she opened the most recent one:

"You are always welcome."

Relief washed over her, followed by a rush of anticipation. Moving in with Boris felt like stepping into a new chapter of her life filled with uncertainty and hope. Immediately, Anika decided she wouldn't tell her parents the whole truth about her plans. Instead, she would keep it simple—leaving the details unsaid.

Eventually, Boris had helped her find a part-time job at a grocery store near his apartment. The manager had been looking for an immediate hire, and Anika saw this as the perfect excuse to justify her decision to leave home. The job gave her a sense of independence and a practical reason to be closer to Boris.

That evening, when her parents came home, she finally broke the news to them.

"I've decided to move out," she announced, keeping her tone firm but calm.

Her parents' reaction was immediate and sharp. "If you leave this house, don't expect to come back. We are warning you," they said, their voices laced with anger and disappointment.

Anika had anticipated their resistance. Their mindset had always been clear—she was supposed to stay under their roof until she got married. That was the only acceptable way to leave home. But Anika couldn't wait for that. She wasn't willing to trade her dreams of freedom and independence for their expectations.

"I understand how you feel," she replied, trying to remain composed though her heart pounded in her chest. "But I've made my decision."

Her parents didn't respond. The tension in the room was palpable, their silence heavy with judgment.

* * *

Later that night, Boris arrived with his car, ready to assist her with the move. He parked outside as Anika gathered her clothes, toiletries, and a few personal belongings. She packed quickly, trying not to dwell on the finality of her actions. As she wheeled her luggage to the front door, her parents stood in the living room, watching her leave without another word. Their disapproval hung in the air, but Anika refused to let it break her resolve.

Boris greeted her with a reassuring smile. "Ready?" he asked, taking one of her bags to load into the trunk.

"Ready," she replied, though a lump formed in her throat as she glanced back at the house one last time.

They drove off into the night, her possessions piled in the back seat. As the distance between her and her childhood home grew, Anika felt a mix of emotions–relief, nervousness, and a flicker of excitement. She was leaving behind the life she had always known to step into something new, something hers.

Boris reached over and held her hand as they drove. "This is your fresh start," he said softly.

Anika nodded, squeezing his hand in return. She didn't know what the future held, but she knew one thing for sure–this was her choice, her life, and her chance to live it on her terms.

Not What It Seems

After a few days, Anika fully settled into her new home. Living with Boris had given her all the freedom she had dreamed of and more. One night, he came home excited about a house party he'd been invited to by some of his classmates. He convinced Anika to come along, and they spent the evening getting ready together. Anika chose a stylish top paired with classic pants, her hair freshly styled into elegant locks. Boris, as usual, looked effortlessly sharp in his casual yet well-fitted outfit. Once they were both ready, they hopped into his car and set off.

As they arrived at the party, the sound of music and muffled laughter greeted them before they even reached the door. A woman opened it, smiling warmly as she welcomed them inside.

The house was unlike anything Anika had ever seen. The lighting was dim and tinged with neon hues, casting the room in an almost surreal glow. The walls were painted a soft pink, and to her surprise, poles were set up in the living room. She noticed several doors leading to other rooms, suggesting this wasn't an ordinary party but something far more indulgent.

As Boris and Anika moved deeper into the crowd, a group of women suddenly swarmed Boris. They giggled and leaned in close, their high-pitched laughter cutting through the music like a knife. The women there wore short skirts that barely covered anything, and some of them wore lingerie.

Anika stood frozen, watching the scene unfold. Confusion prickled at her thoughts, *"Why were these women acting this way? Who were they?"* She tried to piece it together, but the ideas forming in her mind made her stomach churn. *"Are they hookers?"* She thought, as her brow furrowed. *"What kind of party is this?"*

Before she could ask Boris anything, a tall man approached them. He exuded confidence and looked impeccably polished, dressed like a businessman who had just stepped out of a high-profile meeting. Anika thought that he carried himself like he owned the place.

Beside him stood a woman who matched his aura perfectly–sophisticated, poised, and breathtakingly beautiful. Her striking features and elegant attire made her stand out even in the unconventional setting of the party.

Anika's unease deepened as she glanced between the couple and Boris. The tension in her chest grew, and questions swirled in her mind, *"Was this the kind of crowd Boris belonged to? Why had he brought her here?"*

"Heyyy, Boris!" the man called out, striding over. "Long time no see," the man said, clapping Boris on the back. "You know there's always a place for you here."

"Thanks," Boris replied, nervously chuckling as he glanced at Anika. The woman turned to her. "And who's this? Your new *girlfriend?*"

"Yes, she is," Boris said proudly.

"She's gorgeous," the woman said, giving Anika a once-over that made her shift uncomfortably. And it was true–Anika possessed an effortless beauty that turned heads without trying. The woman's smile lingered a little too long. "Welcome, darling. I hope you enjoy yourself."

They left to greet other guests, but the girls remained glued to Boris, their laughter grating on Anika's nerves.

"Excuse me," Anika said firmly, stepping between them and Boris. "Can you give us a moment?"

The women shot her icy looks but moved on.

"Boris, what is this place?" she asked, her voice low and sharp. "Why are these girls walking around half-naked?"

"Some of them are strippers," he admitted casually.

Anika's stomach tightened. Before she could press further, a woman approached her.

"Hi there! My name is Martine," the woman said with a smile.

"Hi," Anika replied curtly, her discomfort palpable.

"First time here, huh? How do you like it?"

"Women walking around half-naked, poles everywhere, old men staring at me like I'm a piece of meat…No, I don't like it," Anika said bluntly.

The woman chuckled. "That was my reaction when I first walked into this brothel."

Anika's eyes widened. "*Brothel?* This is a brothel?"

The woman nodded, unbothered by Anika's shock.

"What do you do here?" Anika asked out of morbid curiosity.

"I'm a sex worker," the woman replied nonchalantly.

"Oh," Anika said, unsurprised but still unsettled.

"What about you?" the woman asked. "What do you do?"

"I'm a cashier," Anika replied. "I just started a part-time job at a grocery store."

The woman raised an eyebrow. "Ever thought about making more money?"

"Not like this," Anika said firmly. "I don't like the atmosphere."

The woman smiled. "I get it. But if you ever change your mind, here's my card. My name's Martine. I'm the coach here."

She handed Anika a sleek business card. "Nice to meet you, Anika."

Anika pocketed the card and looked around, trying to find Boris. He had walked away and was deep in conversation with his friends.

"Boris," she said, leaning in close.

He turned to her with a grin. "Babe, come meet my friends!"

Anika plastered on a fake smile as they greeted her. But when an older man leered at her and asked if she worked there, a wave of disgust boiled inside her. Ignoring him, she turned her attention back to Boris.

"Boris," she whispered, "can we go now?"

"Babe, we just got here," he said, brushing her off. "Relax. Have fun."

"Fine," she snapped. "I'll grab a cab."

Boris watched her walk away, calling after her halfheartedly.

Anika left the party and walked outside. She called a taxi, fuming. "*How could Boris bring me to a place like this?*" she thought.

* * *

When she got back to their apartment, she called Rachel.

"Rachel, you won't believe this," Anika said. "Boris took me to a *brothel.*"

"*What?*! Are you still there?"

"No, I left. But he's still there," Anika said bitterly.

"Break up with him," Rachel said firmly.

Pained by her response, Anika fell silent. She realized that if she broke up with Boris, she would have nowhere to go. Saddened, Anika abruptly ended the call.

"I have to go now Rachel. I'll call you later."

Her emotions were in turmoil. Feeling drained, she took a long, hot shower, hoping the water would wash away the tension. Then, she slipped into bed.

Hours later, Anika heard the familiar sound of a key turning in the lock. Boris entered, moving directly to the bedroom to undress and take a shower. Anika remained still, pretending to be asleep. She was unwilling to engage in any conversation. Instead, Anika focused on keeping her breathing steady, determined to avoid any interaction with him.

* * *

The next morning, Anika woke up and confronted Boris in the kitchen.

"How long have you been going to that place?"

"A year," he admitted.

Frustrated, Anika pushed further. "Did you sleep with any of those women last night?" she asked accusingly.

Boris hesitated, the silence stretching between them. Guilt weighed heavily on him, and he couldn't bring himself to answer. He knew Anika was a good woman—honest, kind, and faithful. The thought of admitting his betrayal made him feel small and ashamed. He couldn't bear to see the hurt in her eyes, so he remained silent, hoping that somehow the truth wouldn't break her heart.

The silence was all Anika needed. It spoke louder than any confession. Her heart ached, but she refused to let him see her break. Without another word, she turned away and began gathering her things, moving with quiet determination. She needed to clear her head, and there was no point in waiting for an apology that might never come. She grabbed her backpack, double-checked her notes for class, and slipped on her coat. Timing was ticking, and she had a bus to catch.

School would at least offer a distraction–a place where her thoughts might settle, even if just for a few hours. As she stepped out of the apartment, the crisp morning air hit her face. She breathed in deeply, willing herself to focus on anything but the silence that had filled the room just moments before.

* * *

After school, Anika braced herself to face Boris. As soon as she got home, he was there waiting. His expression was tense and guarded. Taking a deep breath, he finally spoke.

"Anika, we need to talk," Boris began, his voice flat and detached. "I just wanted to let you know that I have a month-to-month lease for this apartment. There are a couple of weeks left before next month's rent is due, but I won't be renewing my lease. I've been thinking: I really need to focus on my career. I'm struggling to juggle everything, and I think it would be best if we ended our relationship. The apartment came furnished, so I don't have much to take with me. I'll have some friends come by to help me gather my things tonight."

Hearing Boris' words left Anika feeling betrayed. She trusted him, and now he was leaving her. Visibly upset by his decision, Anika nodded with understanding.

However, under no circumstances was she willing to return to her parents' house. Instead, she began to brainstorm ways to take over the lease. Considering her options, she called Rachel, who agreed to stay with her temporarily while she found a better job. Anika felt relieved to have a plan in place.

A few hours later, Boris' friends arrived, ready to help him move. Already packed, Boris began towards the door. Saying goodbye, he leaned in to kiss Anika, but she turned away. It was a sign that they were done for good.

* * *

That evening, Rachel arrived with her usual enthusiasm.

"Forget Boris," Rachel said. "You deserve so much better."

Anika agreed, but was overwhelmed with disappointment. *Now that her relationship with Rob had failed, how was she going to afford rent on her own?* It was then that Rachel noticed a business card on the table—it was the same one Martine had handed Anika the night before.

Picking it up, Rachel laughingly said, "Oh, the *Top Class Ranch*! That's a five-star brothel!"

Anika shook her head. "I can't believe Boris cheated on me. A while ago, he even suggested a *threesome*!? Ugh, I am *so* over him!"

"Good riddance!" Rachel said. "Let's go out and have some fun tonight. How about a nightclub!?"

Anika hesitated but then smiled. "Why not? Let's try it." For the first time in days, she felt a glimmer of excitement.

* * *

Though it was already late, Anika and Rachel got dressed up for a night out. After calling a cab, they headed to *Nudicy Night Club*. The place was buzzing with energy—flashing lights, loud music, and a crowd ready for fun. As they entered, the men turned their heads to compliment the two women. Anika and Rachel exchanged amused smiles and laughed, enjoying the attention.

They started dancing together, letting the music take over. Rachel, ever the social butterfly, mingled effortlessly, but after a while, Anika decided to grab a drink.

At the bar, Anika sought after the bartender, "7UP, please."

As she waited for her drink, a tall, tattooed man with broad shoulders and a deep, smooth voice approached her.

"Hey, gorgeous. You're new here, aren't you? I've never seen you before," he said, flashing a confident smile.

"Yes, it's my first time here," Anika replied, keeping her tone polite but reserved.

The man exuded charm, but an intensity in his gaze made her cautious.

"You seem like someone who knows how to have fun. Want to step outside for a moment? It's quieter," he suggested.

Anika glanced over her shoulder at Rachel, who was still dancing amidst a lively group. "No, I can't leave my friend here alone," she said firmly.

"Fair enough," he said with a shrug, his tone unbothered. Instead of leaving, he gestured toward the far end of the club. "There's a VIP room just over there. It's a bit more private but still part of the party. We can talk there."

"What's in the VIP room?" she asked, her curiosity piqued.

"Special guests like yourself," he said smoothly. "It's got good vibes, and you'll be safe. I promise."

After hesitating for a moment, she nodded. "Okay, just for a couple of minutes."

He led her to the VIP room, holding the door open for her. Inside, the lighting was dim, with a sleek leather couch lining one wall and a small stage in the center. A woman in a red bikini and towering heels stood near the pole, her expression distant.

"Dance for us," the man instructed the stripper casually as he guided Anika to the couch.

The stripper reluctantly moved to the pole and began her routine. Anika felt a pang of discomfort watching the scene unfold. The woman's movements were mechanical, and her lack of enthusiasm was palpable.

"This room's got everything: good music, beautiful women, and the perfect vibe," the man said, lounging beside Anika. "Artists and VIPs love it here."

Anika sipped her drink quietly, her unease growing. As they chatted, the man leaned closer, his voice dropping to a whisper.

"You've never seen a live dance like this before, huh?"

"No, it's my first time," Anika admitted, feeling out of place.

"So, what's a sexy girl like you doing here without a date?" he asked, his tone suggesting.

"I just came to have fun with my friend, Rachel," she replied, shifting away slightly.

Without warning, the man placed a hand on her thigh. Anika froze for a moment before pulling away sharply.

"Excuse me, but I don't appreciate that," she said, standing up firmly. "And I don't like this place. I'm leaving."

She turned to the door, but it wouldn't budge–it was locked. Panic started to creep in. Just then, the door swung open and Rachel stormed in with a bouncer trailing behind her.

"Anika! What's going on!?" Rachel asked, her voice urgent. "Let's go. We can't stay here."

Without a word, Anika followed Rachel out of the VIP room. Once outside the club, Rachel grabbed Anika's hand and led her toward the nearest taxi stand.

"What were you doing with that guy? Do you even know who he is?" Rachel asked, her voice a mix of concern and frustration.

"No," Anika said, still shaken. "I don't know who he is."

"That was Mr. Snake. He's a *pimp*," Rachel revealed in her grave tone.

Anika's stomach dropped. "I had no idea."

"Of course you didn't," Rachel said, exhaling sharply. "They don't exactly advertise it. Thank God I found you. I had to convince the bouncer to tell me where you were. He wouldn't let me in the VIP room until I made a scene."

Anika was ashamed by her ignorance. "Thank you for saving me," she said softly, guilt washing over her.

Rachel squeezed her hand. "I'm just looking out for you, girl."

They flagged down a taxi and rode home in silence, the tension of the night hanging heavily in the air.

Once inside the apartment, Rachel turned to Anika. "Listen, you've got to be more careful. This city is full of people like him."

"I know," Anika said, her voice barely above a whisper. "Thank you for having my back."

Rachel gave her a reassuring smile and hug. "Always. Let's forget about that creep and focus on better nights ahead."

Despite the chaos, they were safe; and that was all that mattered.

Finding Stability

After her breakup with Boris, Anika took a break from school to prioritize her need for financial stability. She'd been working long hours at the local grocery store just a few blocks from her apartment. Her days were filled with the monotony of stacking shelves, ringing up customers, and balancing bills.

Meanwhile, Rachel had been busy preparing for her winter exams. Despite their different routines, the two had enjoyed each other's company. Rachel had been a tremendous emotional and financial support, providing half the rent during her stay. However, it had been thirty days, and it was now time for Rachel to leave. She packed her suitcase, folded clothes, and gathered her books—the reality of her departure settling in. Once finished, she called a cab to pick her up.

"Well, Anika..." Rachel said, standing at the door with her luggage. "If you need anything, I'm just a call away. It's been great living with you. I hope you find a solid job soon. Best of luck, okay?"

"Thank you, Rachel. I appreciate everything," Anika replied, her voice tinged with gratitude.

With a final hug, Rachel stepped outside and got into the waiting taxi. Closing the door behind her, Anika walked to the window, watching as Rachel glanced back at her from the car. Their eyes met briefly before Rachel got inside—the cab eventually disappearing into the city streets.

Watching her drive off, Anika's reality set in: she was alone *again*. The apartment felt emptier than ever. The silence was a stark contrast to the laughter and conversations that had filled it over the past month. She stared at the space where Rachel's belongings had been and took a deep breath. Her mind raced. Rent was due soon, and her grocery store job wasn't cutting it. She needed a solution—and fast.

Anika's gaze shifted to the small business card on the table, which Martine had given her weeks ago. She picked it up, turning it over in her hands. The embossed letters stared back at her, daring her to make a choice. Without overthinking, she grabbed her phone and started dialing.

"Hello, Martine speaking," a voice answered smoothly on the other end.

"Hi, Martine," Anika said, her voice steady but laced with a hint of nervousness. "My name is Anika. We met last month at the brothel with Boris. I've been thinking about what you mentioned before, and I'm interested in joining the business. What should I do to get started?"

There was a pause before Martine responded, her tone filled with intrigue.

"Well, darling, you've made the right choice. Let's meet and discuss the details. I'll walk you through *everything*."

Anika exhaled slowly, gripping the phone tighter. She didn't know exactly what she was stepping into, but one thing was sure—her life was about to change.

CHAPTER 3

Initiation into the World of Prostitution

The next day, Martine introduced Anika to Madam Hayes and her husband, the owners of the prestigious Top Class Ranch. Madam Hayes primarily managed the establishment, as her husband often traveled. Martine reassured Anika that she could choose her clients, offering a sense of control and comfort.

Interestingly, the clientele wasn't limited to individuals; couples frequented the brothel. Martine emphasized that the environment was safe, with strict policies in place to ensure safety. Workers were required to visit a clinic weekly for STD testing to ensure they were healthy. Additionally, it was mandatory to use condoms during all sexual encounters.

The brothel provided flexibility for its workers. Some chose to work there and return home at the end of their shifts, while others lived on-site, fully immersing themselves in the lifestyle. Clients booked appointments through a private website featuring the workers, and all payments were handled upfront before any meetings.

That evening, Anika found herself browsing sex shops and lingerie stores, preparing for her new role. The job description details were a lot to process. *Was she nervous?* Absolutely. The experience of a church girl walking into a sex shop to buy such items was surreal. Anika wasn't entirely sure what she was getting herself into, but she was sure about one thing–she wanted no part of a business where pimps might exploit her. The brothel had a reputation for being safe and professional, which gave her confidence. Legally allowed to make her own choices, this was one she was determined to explore.

Ultimately, Anika's decision to work in the brothel stemmed from two key motivations. First, she desired an income far beyond what her current job could provide (thousands of dollars in a single night). Second, she enjoyed the attention her appearance attracted. She had often been complimented on her beauty and physique. So naturally, these affirmations inspired her to embrace and showcase her body.

Additionally, Martine played a pivotal role in building Anika's confidence. She assured Anika that with the proper guidance, she could become one of the most sought-after workers at the brothel. With Martine's coaching, Anika was determined to transform into a high-class professional, fully prepared to thrive in a new world.

* * *

Anika's first training session with Martine began on Monday. The day was dedicated to perfecting her moves on a dancing pole. Martine spent hours coaching her, emphasizing the importance of grace and confidence. By the end of the session, Anika was exhausted but had made noticeable progress.

Afterward, Martine shifted focus to client interaction, teaching her how to speak seductively and how to captivate attention. They spent hours practicing different communication techniques. Then, Martine assisted Anika with her appearance, exposing her to different beauty treatments.

"For now, don't worry about your hair or nails," Martine advised. "I just want you to be confident in your skin. The rest will come later."

After a full day of training, Anika went to bed exhausted.

* * *

On her second night, Anika had her first trial run with a client. "This one's a regular," Martine informed her. "I'll let you two talk. Have fun, Anika. And remember: keep up the sexy voice, make sure he takes a shower, and always use a CON-DOM. Smile, keep him happy, and you'll do great." With a wink, Martine left Anika to her task.

As Martine had taught her, Anika took the client's hand and led him to her room. Once inside, she locked the door behind them.

"Hi, I'm Anika," she said warmly, offering her hand for a handshake.

"I'm Dave," he replied.

"You can go ahead and take a shower. I'll be ready when you're done," Anika instructed.

Dave emerged from the bathroom a few minutes later, wrapped in a towel.

"So, what do you do for a living?" Anika asked, trying to make conversation.

"I'm a lawyer," he answered casually. "I come here once in a while. Work keeps me so busy that I barely have time to date. This place is convenient–I get what I need, and then return to my life."

"I see," Anika said, genuinely surprised. She hadn't expected a lawyer to be one of her clients. Martine had been right–this wasn't a place frequented only by stereotypical "creeps."

"You look shocked," Dave laughed, noticing Anika's wide eyes. "Is it because I'm a lawyer? You'd be surprised at the kind of people who come here. This brothel is top-class. Lawyers, doctors, business executives–we're all here to unwind. Most of us are too busy to maintain relationships. This place is professional and discreet, which is why I keep coming back." He paused, his gaze steady. "You *are* of legal age, right?" he asked, his tone suddenly more serious.

"Yes, of course. I'm actually turning twenty-one soon," Anika replied confidently.

Dave nodded in relief–thankful that Canadian laws were clear about age limits.

As they continued their conversation, Anika gently rubbed Dave's thigh to build intimacy. The atmosphere shifted as they started to kiss, their interaction growing more passionate. Dave's hands explored her body, squeezing her breasts as he leaned down to kiss them. Anika responded by reaching for his towel. Her fingers brushed against his skin as she slowly pulled it away, letting it fall to the floor. She retrieved a condom and helped him put it on before kneeling to perform oral sex. Afterward, she climbed onto him, and they proceeded to have intercourse.

When they finished, Dave glanced at his watch. "I've got to run. I have a client meeting in twenty minutes," he said, hastily getting dressed. "Thanks for the great time."

As he prepared to leave, Anika felt a mix of emotions. Her first experience was behind her, and she couldn't deny the confidence it had given her. She was starting to understand this new world, one step at a time.

Anika helped him get dressed, picking up his vest from the chair and handing it to him.

"Thank you for the service, Anika. You were great," he said with a smile before leaving the room.

Anika closed the door and sat on the edge of the bed. She exhaled deeply. "*Well,*" she thought to herself, "*it wasn't terrible: a blow job in twenty minutes!*"

After the lawyer's departure, Anika headed straight to the shower. As the water cascaded over her, she fell into deep reflection. She felt an overwhelming sense of discomfort. Inside, she felt unclean, disgusted by the thought of having sex with a stranger. The experience left her feeling disconnected from herself. "*Where was that confidence I was supposed to have?*" she wondered. Snapping back to reality, she glanced at the clock. It was noon–time to head to the lobby.

All the women were expected to gather there to meet a new client. The routine was simple: the girls would form a lineup, allowing the client to take their time and carefully select who they wanted to spend time with.

As the client entered the lobby, he strolled down the lineup, pausing to interact with each woman. He seemed intent on getting to know them before making his decision. After a few moments of deliberation, he stopped and turned to Martine. "I choose her," he said, gesturing toward Anika. "She is *gorgeous*," he added, his eyes fixed on her.

Anika felt her heart race as Martine smiled approvingly. It was her turn *again*. She knew she had to step into the role, even as she wrestled with the emotions swirling within her.

"Well, if she's your choice, then she's all yours!" Martine said with a smile.

Anika stepped forward, took the client by the hand, and led him to her room. Once inside, she gently closed the door behind him and sat down on the bed, motioning for him to make himself comfortable.

The client removed his jacket and looked around. "You can put it on the chair," Anika suggested. He complied, hanging the coat neatly before she spoke again.

"Why don't you take a quick shower to freshen up?" she said with a warm smile.

He agreed, and later emerged from the bathroom wearing a robe. Then he sat beside Anika on the bed.

"So," Anika began, her tone light and conversational, "what made you decide to come here?"

The client sighed, his expression softening. "Well, I'm a doctor with over twenty years of experience. I live alone—my wife passed away several years ago. I've never remarried and, honestly, my work keeps me busy. I barely have time for anything else. Coming here allows me to unwind and meet beautiful girls like you."

Anika nodded, attentively listening as he continued.

"I've never seen you here before," he remarked, studying her face. "This must be your first time. Am I right?"

"It is," Anika admitted, her voice steady despite her nerves. "Today is my first day working here."

"Well," he said with a small smile, "I hope you'll make it memorable. I've heard great things about you already. I love girls who take their work seriously."

His eyes lingered on her chest, clearly drawn to her figure. Anika wore a push-up bra that accentuated her bosom, and she noticed his gaze.

Smiling subtly, she leaned in, took his hands, and kissed him softly on the lips.

Their encounter quickly escalated, and they engaged in sexual intercourse, using a condom as required. This session lasted about thirty minutes. At one point, the doctor asked her to use handcuffs and a whip during their time together. Anika found the request amusing, but she kept her composure and complied with his wishes. The playful interaction led to laughter and excitement, and they concluded the session with a sense of intimacy.

When they were finished, Anika helped him get dressed.

"Wow," he said, adjusting his shirt. "You're good at this. I'll be back to see you soon."

"Thank you, Doctor," Anika replied with a polite smile.

"Please, call me Albert," he said warmly.

"Alright, Albert," she responded, her voice smooth. "See you next time at the Top Class Ranch."

* * *

Later that day, Martine knocked on Anika's door and stepped inside.

"Hey, Anika, want some pizza? Madam Hayes just ordered a bunch of boxes for you girls. They're in the lobby–help yourself!"

"Thanks," Anika said, getting up. She took a quick shower, put on a comfortable robe, and headed out to grab a slice of pizza.

As she was eating, Martine approached her with a stack of papers. "We'll meet with the other girls soon," Martine informed her. "Another client will be arriving in a couple of minutes. In the meantime, here's your schedule for the week. It includes all your appointments. It is very important that you keep this with you."

Anika took the printed sheet and scanned it briefly. "Got it," she said, tucking it away. She knew her journey at the Top Class Ranch had only just begun.

Anika glanced at the schedule in her hand and saw she had an appointment at 6 p.m. with a couple. Her eyes scanned the names: *Mishka Rodriguez* and *Shawn Jestics*.

Her heart nearly stopped. "*Oh my gosh. Shawn Jestics?!*" she thought, her pulse quickening. "*He's one of my favorite rappers! Am I really meeting him, with his girlfriend, Mishka?*"

A wave of nervousness swept over her, and Martine, noticing her reaction, offered a reassuring smile. "I know you've got this," she said, placing a hand on Anika's shoulder.

Just then, Madam Hayes emerged from her office, addressing the sex workers gathered in the lobby. Some were still munching on pizza.

"Alright, ladies! I hope everyone is doing well tonight. I brought some food so that you can keep your energy up. You're all doing fantastically. And Anika, thank you for joining us—we're glad to have you on board. Enjoy your meal and have a great evening ladies!" With a warm smile, Madam Hayes returned to her office.

As the night approached, the girls began preparing for their upcoming clients. Anika chose a red lingerie set, applied her best makeup, and topped it off with bold red lipstick. She slipped into a pair of high heels, her heart pounding as she got ready.

Yet, as she prepared, doubts crept into her mind. She felt small waves of guilt. "*Should I go back to my old cashier job at the grocery store?*" she wondered. "*Maybe I should call my parents for help...*" Before she could delve deeper into her thoughts, the next client arrived.

The girls lined up to greet him as he entered the lobby. From the back of the line, Anika couldn't make out what he looked like. Especially because his hat obscured his face. As he approached closer and removed his hat, Anika's stomach dropped. It was *Denis Roaster,* one of the elders from her church.

"*No way. Really!?*" Anika's mind reeled. "*What is he doing here?*" She lowered her head, overwhelmed by embarrassment and shame. Denis was a husband and father of five. "*Why couldn't he stay home and make love to his wife instead of coming here?*" Anika thought angrily.

"Welcome to the Top Class Ranch, Mr. Roaster," Martine said warmly.

"Thank you for having me," Denis replied with a smile.

Anika felt like throwing up. She avoided eye contact as Denis began to look over the lineup. When his eyes landed on her, she shot him a piercing '*if you pick me, I'll kill you*' glare. Recognizing her immediately, he did his best to hide his embarrassment. He quickly moved on and chose someone else. The selected girl took Denis by the hand and led him to her room.

Yet, Anika was still shaken. "*A husband and father of five...*" she thought bitterly. "*And an elder in the church, no less.*" She couldn't believe what she had just witnessed. Denis's wife was a beautiful woman with a sweet demeanor. *How could he betray her like this?*

Feeling overwhelmed, Anika stepped outside for some fresh air. She gazed at the sky, trying to sort through her thoughts. "*Is this something I can keep doing?*" she wondered. "*Working at a brothel might bring me the money I need, but it's not the life I want. It doesn't make me happy.*"

She stayed outside, lost in thought for nearly an hour. When she finally decided to head back inside, she saw Denis leaving the brothel. As he passed her, he suddenly reached out and grabbed her arm.

"What are you doing here, *little girl?*" he asked, his voice tinged with disapproval.

"Don't touch me," Anika snapped, snatching her arm back. "What are *you* doing here?"

"Do your parents know you're working here?" he countered, ignoring her question.

Anika held his gaze but said nothing.

He leaned in closer, lowering his voice. "If you tell anyone at church that I was here–*anyone*, including your parents–it won't end well for you. Do you hear me?" His tone carried a thinly veiled threat.

She froze as his face moved closer to her ear. "You keep my secret, and I'll keep yours," he whispered. "Your parents don't even know you're here, *do they?*"

Before she could react, Denis straightened up satisfied. Then he tapped her shoulder with a smug smile, and walked away, leaving Anika standing there in stunned silence. Anika couldn't shake her curiosity about why he had come to the brothel. She went back inside, her thoughts racing.

At the bar, Maya, the worker who had just been with the elder, was sipping on a drink. Anika hesitated for a moment before walking over.

"Hey…Maya," she said, her voice steady but tinged with nervousness.

"Hey, Anika! What's up?" Maya replied, flashing her a warm smile.

"Listen," Anika began, lowering her voice and glancing around to ensure no one was listening, "just curious–did that man tell you why he came here?"

Maya raised an eyebrow. "Oh, you mean the older guy? The one you were just talking to? Why? Do you know him?"

"Yes…" Anika admitted reluctantly.

Maya tilted her head, intrigued. "Okay. What do you want to know about him?"

"Whatever he might have told you," Anika replied softly, trying to mask her eagerness.

"Well," Maya began, swirling her drink lazily, "he's married. He told me something about not getting the variety he wanted in bed. His wife, apparently, is only interested in the missionary position. He wanted to try different things and that's understandable. I mean, some men just aren't sexually satisfied. They feel unfulfilled at home. Honestly, I see a lot of married men here. And most of them have the same excuses for cheating on their wives: boring sex or no sex at all." She smirked, shrugging. "But hey, that's why we're here, right? We're not here to counsel them. I gave him what he wanted, and he left satisfied."

While Maya spoke about Elder Denis, Anika's mind wandered. Her thoughts shifted to her parents. She realized they hadn't seemed affectionate in years. She couldn't remember when she saw them kiss or hold hands. *Was that normal? Was that what marriage boiled down to— emptiness and routine?*

Then Anika's thoughts turned to her almost-marriage to Rob. She remembered his arrogance, the way he believed he could do whatever he pleased without consequence. If they'd married, would her life have been a nightmare? Anika shuddered at the thought, realizing she'd dodged a bullet.

Still, the sight of Elder Denis at the brothel saddened her. A man who once preached about faith and family had fallen into this shadowy world, chasing fulfillment he couldn't find at home. Overwhelmed with thought, Anika glanced at the clock and snapped out of her reflection. It was time to prepare for her next appointment—*Shawn Jestics*. He was finally in town.

* * *

Shawn walked into the brothel with his girlfriend by his side an hour later. Anika's heart raced as she saw him. He was even more attractive in person than on TV. She couldn't believe she was about to meet him.

However, his girlfriend's presence complicated things. If Anika rejected her, she'd have to reject Shawn too—that was the rule. Yet, a part of her desperately wanted this chance. Shawn had been her celebrity crush for years, and now he was standing right in front of her.

Swallowing her nerves, Anika took both their hands and led them to the room. Her mind swirled with a mix of anticipation and disbelief.

As the woman entered the room, she smiled and said, "Hmm, it smells so good here."

"Thank you," Anika replied politely.

The man undressed, revealing tattoos sprawling across his muscular frame. When he smiled, his dimples appeared, giving him a boyish charm. Meanwhile, the quieter and more reserved woman started to remove her clothes as she watched her partner.

Anika decided to break the ice by directing her attention to the woman. "So, what made you choose this brothel?"

The man answered, "Ah, my girlfriend doesn't speak much English— mostly speaks Spanish."

"Oh!" Anika responded with a light laugh. "My Spanish isn't great, unfortunately."

"No worries," the man said, chuckling. "We picked this place because we know it's a five-star brothel. It's known for hosting people like us who expect the best. We've only been in town for a couple of days, but we were intrigued when we saw your profile on the website. It said you're 'new and very talented.' And now that I see you in person, I can say they weren't wrong—you're stunning. We just had to meet you."

His compliments made Anika smile nervously, but she managed to keep her composure. Once the couple was fully undressed, the man suddenly lifted Anika off her feet and tossed her onto the bed. Startled, she froze momentarily, worried that things might get rough. He climbed onto the bed, kissing her passionately and trailing his lips down her body. His actions grew more aggressive as he tore off her bra and underwear, catching Anika completely off guard.

At that moment, the woman leaned in and kissed Anika's neck. Uncomfortable, Anika pulled back slightly and said without thinking, "I'm sorry, but I don't want to be touched by a woman." Immediately regretting her words, Anika thought, *Mama, business is business.* With a sincere apology, she pushed her feelings aside and allowed the woman to continue. Anika did her best to pretend she enjoyed the kisses trailing across her body. The wild session lasted an exhausting 1.5 hours. The man was shockingly energetic, leaving Anika feeling more drained than she expected.

When it was over, the couple quickly got dressed. As the woman adjusted her outfit, she glanced at Anika and said, "Tu lencería es barata, tienes que comprar un atuendo más lujoso."

Anika frowned slightly. "What did she say?" she asked the man confusingly.

He chuckled and translated, "She said your lingerie looks cheap, and you should get something more luxurious."

The man pulled out his wallet, handed her three hundred dollars, and added with a grin, "*Here.* Treat yourself to something nice."

"Thanks," Anika said, accepting the money.

"Well, lady, it's been fun. Thanks for having us," he said, giving his girlfriend a playful slap on her rear.

"Thank you for visiting the brothel," Anika replied with a forced smile.

As the couple left, Anika sat back on the bed and sighed. So much for meeting her *'crush.'* The experience had left her feeling worse than before–disconnected, unfulfilled, and, above all, tired.

Work Hard, Play Hard

Finally, her shift was over. Anika headed to Madam Hayes's office to check out.

"So, Miss Anika," Madam Hayes asked warmly. "How was your first day at the brothel?"

Anika hesitated, choosing her words carefully. "A bit awkward. I ran into some challenges," she admitted.

"That's normal, hun. It's part of the process. Remember, Martine is an excellent coach–she can teach you how to handle tricky situations and build confidence. Don't hesitate to reach out if you need anything. We're here for you."

"Thank you," Anika replied, appreciating the kindness.

"Oh, and here's your pay for the night–three thousand dollars. Not bad for a first day, huh?" Madam Hayes said, sliding an envelope across the desk.

Anika's eyes widened. "Thank you so much!" she exclaimed, unable to hide her excitement.

"You earned it. Now get some rest, and I'll see you tomorrow, alright?"

"Absolutely. See you tomorrow."

Anika left the office, clutching the envelope tightly. Finally, she could pay her rent and even splurge on a few things she wanted. But the exhaustion from the night weighed heavily on her. *Was it all worth it?*

* * *

Back at home, Anika resolved to go to bed early. She still had her other job to attend to in the morning–working at the grocery store. Yet, juggling two jobs would not last forever. The brothel was far more lucrative, and she no longer saw the need to work at both. The long mornings of waking early only to stand at a cash register felt unnecessary now that her evenings brought in more money than she'd ever earned at the store.

It wasn't long before Anika decided to quit her cashier job. In just a few weeks, she had become one of the brothel's most sought-after workers. Couples booked appointments to explore their fantasies with her; older men came seeking her beauty and charm. Even women expressed interest, drawn to her allure. Over the course of a month, Anika had slept with hundreds of clients–both men and women.

During this time, Martine had taken her under her wing. She coached her on perfecting her craft, boosting her confidence, and teaching her how to handle complex or unusual requests. As a result, Anika basked in the compliments from her clients. She felt influential, desired, and admired. *"Who could resist me?"* she often thought, looking at herself in the mirror, adorned in her upgraded designer lingerie and carefully applied makeup.

With the steady income, Anika was able to live the life she had only dreamed of before. Her rent and phone bills were paid with ease. She bought luxurious clothes, high-end makeup, and accessories that she had never imagined she could afford. Nights out with new friends became routine–shopping sprees, parties, and fancy dinners filled her free time. On the surface, she was living the spicy, glamorous life she had always craved.

However, something still gnawed at her from the inside. Despite the success, compliments, and money, she felt an emptiness she couldn't explain. Late at night, after the music and laughter faded, a quiet sadness would creep into her thoughts. She couldn't pinpoint what it was, but it lingered–a desire for more–a whisper of something missing.

Occasionally, she'd receive messages from folks at church, asking how she was doing and urging her to return. Seeing their words filled her with guilt, but she did her best to push them aside.

Although she tried, she couldn't hide her thoughts about her siblings, whom she had helped care for growing up. She loved them deeply, and they had always looked up to her. The thought of them–or worse, her parents–discovering her work terrified her. She knew the truth could tear them apart. Though her heart ached at their disappointment, she couldn't leave this new life. For now, she buried those feelings under layers of lipstick, laughter, and late-night escapades: *this* was the life she'd chosen.

Party Gone Wrong

One evening, Anika was on her way home after a quick stop at a deli store. As she walked the streets, she ran into James, a regular client she had worked with at Top Class Ranch. James had just returned from a trip to Russia and was now back in the city with his partner.

"Hey, James," Anika greeted, giving him a polite smile.

"Anika!" James responded enthusiastically. "We're heading to a party at my hotel room. Want to join us?"

"Hmm, maybe. What time is the party?" she asked.

"Right now," James said with a grin. Pulling out his phone, he offered to text Anika the address.

Curious and unsure, Anika complied. After saying goodbye, she went home to change into something appropriate for the party. Then she took a cab to the hotel.

When she arrived at James's room, the "party" wasn't what she expected. There was music playing, but the room was only occupied by James and his partner. Anika realized quickly that James' partner was likely his boyfriend. That's when she began to piece the situation together. She suspected they had invited her for a threesome, but the idea didn't sit well with her. Anika wasn't in the mood for anything sexual tonight.

The two men looked her up and down as she entered.

"Hey, *lil' girl.* Want to have some *fun?*" James' partner asked, smirking.

Anika bristled at the term but chose not to respond, keeping her composure.

"Want to dance for us?" the partner followed up.

"I didn't come here to dance," Anika said flatly. "I thought this was going to be an actual party."

"It is," James interjected with a sly grin. "And you're the star of it. Don't worry–you'll be paid for your time."

Anika hesitated but decided to stay. After all, there were only two people. She thought, *"Maybe it wouldn't hurt to entertain them briefly..."* Closing the door behind her, she placed her handbag on the couch.

"Fine. Just pick a different song, okay?" she said reluctantly.

The men agreed, and immediately a new song began to play. Listening to the music, Anika started to move, swaying her hips. Almost immediately, James' partner pulled out his phone and began filming her.

"Hey!" Anika said sharply. "I'm not comfortable being filmed. This is private."

James gave her a reassuring smile, though it didn't ease the tension. "Don't worry about him," he said, reaching for her hand and motioning for her to sit on his lap.

Reluctantly, she sat, straddling him as she danced. His hands gripped her waist, and his partner continued to film despite her earlier objection.

Anika turned to the man with the camera. "I said *no filming*. Put the phone away," she said firmly.

Before she could rise, James took hold of her face, turning it toward him. "Relax," he said with a grin. "It's time to have some fun." Immediately, he tried pushing Anika's head down toward his crotch.

Anika pulled away, glaring at him. **"Don't do that**," she said, her voice low but firm.

James persisted, trying again to force her head down.

Anika stood abruptly, brushing off his hands. "My business is meant for pleasure," she said, her tone icy. "And I have every right to refuse unwanted behavior. Don't cross that line again."

James's grin faded. Likewise, his partner lowered the camera, sensing the tension in the room.

Anika picked up her handbag and walked toward the door. "You need to understand boundaries, James. You don't treat people like this."

She left the room without another word, stepping into the cool night air. As the city lights sparkled around her, she felt a mix of anger and disappointment. Anika stood outside the door for a moment trying to gain her composure. No amount of money was worth compromising her dignity.

Back in the room, James's expression darkened as Anika's refusal echoed. He gestured sharply for his partner to stop filming. Finally, he called out to Anika and said, "You don't tell me *no*." Low and menacingly, James went outside and grabbed her by the arms. "When I want something, I GET IT. So, **give it to me!**"

Before Anika could react, James pulled her back into the room and pushed her to the floor. Slamming the door behind him, his force left Anika momentarily stunned.

"Turn off the camera, Walton!" he barked at his partner, who hesitated before reluctantly complying.

James towered over Anika, his eyes filled with a mix of anger and entitlement. She tried to get up, but he shoved her back down, pinning her to the floor. Panic surged through her as he started pulling at her clothing, scratching her roughly.

"Get off me!" she yelled, struggling against his grip. Her heart pounded as she realized the precariousness of her situation. She fought back, twisting and pushing, but his weight bore down on her. Then, James rolled Anika over on her stomach, making it nearly impossible to break free. Her fear escalated when she felt him lift her dress. She screamed, but her voice muffled against the carpet.

"*No! Stop it!*" she cried, her voice breaking.

James ignored her, his breathing coming in heavy, erratic gasps. Anika's mind raced, searching for a way to stop him, but the sexual assault was quick and brutal. When he was finally satisfied, James rolled off her. Anika scrambled to her feet, shaking with rage and terror. She glared at James, who lay on the floor, panting and seemingly oblivious to the devastation he had caused.

Anika adjusted her dress, her hands trembling. "*You don't get to do this,*" she spat, her voice raw with emotion. "You think you can treat people like this and get away with it? You're *disgusting*."

Walton stood frozen near the corner of the room, his phone now at his side. He looked down, avoiding Anika's gaze. Anika picked up her handbag and stormed out of the room. Her heart pounded with a mix of fear, anger, and humiliation. As she stepped into the night air, the cool breeze did little to calm the storm inside her.

Walking away from the hotel, she knew one thing: she couldn't let this go unanswered. Her body was trembling. The reality of what had just happened sank in like a crushing weight. She had been violated.

As Anika struggled to process the shock, she heard Walton urge from behind her, "James, let's go!" Eyeing her on the way out, the two men fled the hotel room, slamming the door behind them.

Anika was left alone, while the music from the hotel still blared from the room. The rhythm pounded against the walls, but it was as though the world had gone silent to her. Her body ached, her clothes were torn, and a sharp pain reminded her of the blood she could feel between her legs. Anika tried to move but collapsed onto the cement parking lot, her strength sapped by shock and trauma. She stared at the ceiling, her mind racing yet frozen, replaying the nightmare she had just endured.

After a few minutes, sheer will propelled her forward. Crawling towards her purse that had fallen beside her, Anika reached in and began looking for her phone. Her hands shook violently when she found it, barely managing to press the numbers.

"9-1-1, what's your emergency?" came the calm voice on the other end.

Anika's voice quivered as she whispered, "I…I've been assaulted. I need help. *Please.*"

The dispatcher immediately responded, "Help is on the way. Can you tell me where you are?"

Anika gave the hotel's name and room number as best as possible, her words faltering but clear enough for the dispatcher to understand.

"You're safe now," the dispatcher assured her. "Stay on the line with me. Officers and medical help are on their way."

Anika clutched her phone tightly, tears streaming down her face. Though her body felt broken and her spirit battered, she had taken the first step toward seeking justice. When the ambulance arrived, the paramedics carefully helped Anika onto the stretcher. She was physically weak and emotionally shattered, her mind replaying the traumatic events over and over. The ride to the hospital was a blur, punctuated by flashes of concern in the paramedics' voices.

* * *

Anika spent the entire night in the hospital. Doctors and nurses came in and out of the room, asking questions, running tests, and offering words of comfort that felt distant and hollow. Anika barely responded. She felt as if the walls were closing in, her sense of self crumbling under the weight of helplessness and despair.

She couldn't stop the dark thoughts creeping in. *Would it be better to end it all?* She felt isolated, betrayed by the world, and utterly alone. Her life felt out of control, spiraling further with each moment. And to make it all worse, the sting of Boris breaking up with her resurfaced, compounding her anguish. *"Will I ever find love?"* she wondered, staring at her reflection in the hospital room's small mirror. Her face was pale, her eyes hollow and sunken. She could barely recognize herself.

A Cry For Help

Weeks passed in a haze of exhaustion. At the hospital, Anika refused to eat much, her appetite stolen by the trauma. After all the adrenaline had passed, her body felt foreign to her, weighed down by weakness. Each trip to the bathroom was agonizing–her urine burned with every attempt. She cried quietly in her hospital bed, feeling like a shell of the person she once was. Meanwhile, the doctors ran tests and tried to figure out why she wasn't getting better.

Anika realized she couldn't endure this pain alone any longer. Reaching for the phone by her bed, she dialed Rachel, her voice trembling as she spoke.

"Rachel...I need you," she pleaded.

"Hey, Anika," Rachel responded, her tone hurried. "I can't talk right now, I'm still working. My boss is–"

"I need you **now**, Rachel," Anika interrupted, her voice cracking.

"What's wrong? Why do you sound like this, Anika?"

"I'm not feeling well..." she admitted, hesitating. "And my vagina burns whenever I pee."

There was a pause. "*Whoa*...where are you?"

"I'm at Hope Hospital. I, I was raped..."

Silence filled the line. Rachel didn't respond immediately; the weight of Anika's words sank in. Then, without another word, Rachel hung up. Anika stared at the phone in disbelief, her heart sinking further. She tried calling Rachel back, but there was no answer. Her chest tightened with the fear that Rachel would abandon her in her time of need.

Then her phone buzzed with a text:

"**I'm on the way**," it read.

Anika felt a small glimmer of hope for the first time in days. It wasn't much, but it was enough to keep her going. Rachel had always been a loyal friend to Anika—the kind of person willing to drop everything to be there when it mattered most. Whether it meant missing work, skipping class, or rearranging her life, Rachel never hesitated when Anika needed her. It was refreshing to see her loyalty hadn't changed.

When Rachel finally arrived at the hospital, she was greeted by the sight of Anika, frail and struggling to move. Anika attempted to stand but could barely keep her balance. She moved slowly toward Rachel, her legs trembling beneath her.

"Anika! It's me," Rachel said, rushing to her friend.

Before Anika could take two steps toward her, she collapsed into Rachel's arms. Rachel caught her, holding her tightly and guiding her back to the bed.

"Anika, are you okay?" Rachel asked, her voice trembling with worry. Tears welled up in her eyes as she looked at her friend's pale, feverish face.

Anika shook her head weakly. Before she could answer, her stomach churned violently. She leaned over the side of the bed and vomited onto the floor.

"Okay...that's it. I'm calling a nurse," Rachel said, panicking as she pressed the emergency button.

Within minutes, a nurse entered the room, taking control of the situation. "Miss, I need you to step outside for a moment," the nurse firmly told Rachel. "Your friend needs to rest."

Reluctantly, Rachel left the room but stayed nearby, pacing in the hallway until a doctor approached her.

"Are you here for Ms. Anika Bailes?" the doctor asked as he approached Rachel.

"Yes. I'm Anika's friend, Rachel," she said anxiously.

The doctor's expression was serious. "Anika gave me permission to speak with you. She has tested positive for gonorrhea. Her symptoms–burning urination, vomiting, and fever–are all signs of an infection from unprotected sex. She's also severely dehydrated, and her condition requires immediate treatment. She won't be able to return to work until she fully recovers. We're administering antibiotics and fluids to stabilize her."

Rachel's heart sank. "Oh no...she's been through so much already," she whispered, tears in her eyes.

The doctor hesitated before adding, "That's not all. Over the last few days, we've conducted several blood tests. Anika may be pregnant."

Rachel's eyes widened in shock. "*Pregnant?* Oh my God..." She placed her hand over her mouth, overwhelmed by the news.

The doctor nodded. "We'll confirm the results once all the tests are completed. In the meantime, we'll continue to monitor her condition closely."

Rachel leaned against the wall for support, her mind racing. She felt a mixture of fear, anger, and sadness for her friend. More than anything, she knew she had to be strong for Anika. Whatever happened next, she wouldn't let her go through it alone.

* * *

When Rachel later returned to Anika's hospital bedside, she sat beside her and gently broke the news. "Anika, the doctor confirmed it: you're pregnant."

Anika's whole world seemed to freeze. She stared at Rachel, her face pale and blank. A *baby? Now?* Was she even remotely ready to have a child? Her heart raced as the weight of the news settled in her chest.

Rachel placed a reassuring hand on Anika's arm and continued, "Listen, you're not alone in this. The doctor said that your baby can still be healthy with proper treatment. You'll need to follow up with all your appointments and take your medications to prevent complications like miscarriage or premature birth. I will stay with you for a week and help you get through this, but after that, I must return to work."

Anika nodded weakly. Her mind was a blur of emotions–fear, guilt, and uncertainty. She couldn't imagine herself as a mother, not in her current state. The news was too much to handle.

* * *

When Anika had fully recovered and was released from the hospital, Rachel helped her settle back into her apartment. The two friends spent the evening discussing Anika's health and plans for the baby. Anika decided she would follow the doctor's advice and commit to her treatments, but deep down, she couldn't shake the feeling of being unprepared and overwhelmed.

That night, while Rachel cooked dinner, she broke the silence. "So...you went to a party in that guy's hotel room?"

Anika hesitated before answering, "It wasn't supposed to be like this. I just needed a break, something to take my mind off everything. I thought I knew him. I realize now that I was wrong."

Rachel sighed, her frustration evident. The last few days, Anika had filled Rachel in on all the details regarding her sex work. It was a lot for Rachel to process. "This is crazy, Anika. Working at a brothel, sleeping with all kinds of people, and now you're telling me you've been with women too? Does this mean you're *bisexual?*"

By now, Rachel had finished cooking and had set Anika's plate in front of her. She stared down at the food quietly. Though Rachel was a great cook and had prepared a delicious meal, Anika didn't have much of an appetite. The conversation made her stomach turn, as she remembered the mistake she had made. She forced herself to take small bites, but Anika didn't have the energy or the words to defend her choices.

Rachel softened her tone. "Look, I'm not here to judge you. I want you to think about your future, especially now that a baby is involved. I wish I could offer you more financial assistance, but my job has no openings until next year. You need to find a safer way to earn a living–one that won't put you or your baby at risk."

Anika finally looked up at Rachel, tears forming in her eyes. "I don't know where to go, Rachel. My life feels like a mess. How do I even begin to fix this?"

Rachel sat down beside her, pulling her into a comforting hug. "One step at a time, Anika. You're stronger than you think, and you're not alone. We'll figure it out together."

Picking Up the Pieces

A week after Rachel returned to town, Anika found herself alone (again), trying to piece her life back together. She attended her doctor's appointments but didn't return to the brothel. She couldn't bear the thought of going back to that life, not after everything that had happened.

When she finally had the strength to call Madam Hayes, she explained her situation: her pregnancy, her STD, and her inability to continue working. Madam Hayes offered a few polite words of understanding but made it clear that there was no place for her at the brothel under these circumstances.

Disappointed by her response, Anika felt trapped. She couldn't go back to her parents–they didn't even know she had been sexually active, let alone raped and pregnant. The thought of their judgment terrified her. She wasn't financially stable, and knew that deep down, that she wasn't ready to raise a child. Anika grew desperate for a way out.

As weeks passed, her situation grew more overwhelming. At six weeks pregnant, Anika finally made a painful decision. She couldn't see a future where she could provide for her child. She had always considered herself pro-life, but now, faced with her circumstances, she realized the weight of such a choice. She decided to have an abortion.

* * *

Sitting in the clinic, Anika's hands trembled as she signed the necessary forms. The nurse led her to the exam room, where the doctor gently explained the procedure and conducted an ultrasound. The conversation lasted about ten minutes, but it felt like a lifetime. Hearing the baby's heartbeat on the screen was a painful reminder of the outcome of her attack. She couldn't bear the thought of living with this consequence for the rest of her life. Abortion was the only answer that made sense to her. She was ready to undergo the surgery.

After the procedure, Anika was taken to a recovery room to rest. She felt a flood of emotions–relief, sadness, and an overwhelming sense of loss. She hadn't been prepared for how deeply the abortion would affect her. The reality of what she had just lost hit her like a tidal wave. Tears streamed down her face as the doctor explained that she still had a strong chance of having children in the future, but her mind was already racing. *"Do I even want to have kids after this abortion?"* she wondered. She had heard stories of women struggling with fertility after abortions, and the thought terrified her.

As she sat in the recovery room, Anika felt like she had been split into two. Part of her knew she had made the only choice she could under the circumstances, but another part of her mourned the miracle she had just let go. She eventually left the clinic feeling hollow, the sight of the ultrasound running through her mind. Taking in the scenery outside, she let out a deep breath. The world outside seemed unchanged, but Anika knew she would never be the same.

CHAPTER 4
An Unexpected Encounter

In the months that followed, Anika sought help through trauma therapy, determined to heal from the devastating experiences of rape and abortion. Now that she was no longer working and focusing on her therapy, Anika used her savings to help her stay financially afloat. Before, Anika had been earning around $7,500 a month working at the Top Class Ranch. The money was sufficient to cover rent and meet her basic needs, with plenty left over for other expenses. Generous tips from professionals and occasional celebrity endorsements boosted her income, enabling her to build a solid emergency fund that covered months of expenses.

Recovery was a long and painful journey, but therapy offered her the opportunity to confront her emotions and process the trauma. One of the most valuable lessons she learned was the importance of regulating her nervous system. Engaging in art became a vital tool in this process—something that came naturally to Anika. Sketching and painting allowed her to channel her pain into creativity, offering both solace and a sense of control amidst the chaos of her emotions. Art became an integral part of Anika's everyday life.

* * *

One day, she found herself alone at the Blooming Café, a local coffee shop. Sitting at a table with her sketchbook open in front of her, her pencil moved freely across the page. The rhythmic scratching of graphite against paper was soothing, a small escape from the heaviness that often lingered in her thoughts.

Just as she was beginning to lose herself in the flow of drawing, her focus broke. A man caught her attention. He wasn't making any effort to conceal his curiosity, his gaze shifting between her face and the sketchbook. Anika felt a flicker of self-consciousness and quickly looked back down at her work, pretending not to notice. She hoped he wouldn't approach her. This was *her time*—a rare moment of solitude and peace that she desperately needed. But moments later, she saw him walking toward her. He was holding a cup of coffee, his steps casual but deliberate. Anika felt her shoulders tense.

"What does *he* want?" she thought, glancing up briefly.

"Hi," he said with a warm smile. His voice was calm, not pushy. "Sorry to interrupt. I couldn't help but notice your drawing. You're talented."

Anika blinked, unsure how to respond. "Uh...thanks," she said, her voice quiet.

"May I?" he gestured to the empty chair across from her.

She hesitated. Part of her wanted to send him away, but there was something disarming about his demeanor. "Sure," she said reluctantly.

He set his coffee down and sat, leaning slightly forward to look at her sketchbook. "Wow, you've got a lot of emotion in your work. It's *raw*...honest."

Anika glanced at her pages, suddenly feeling exposed. Her drawings were her outlet, reflecting her pain and frustration. She hadn't intended for anyone to see them. "I guess," she murmured, closing the book slightly.

"I'm sorry," he said quickly. "I didn't mean to pry. I'm John, by the way." He extended his hand.

"Anika," she replied, shaking his hand briefly.

John nodded, his gaze steady but kind. "Nice to meet you, Anika. I didn't mean to intrude. I just...well, I'm an artist too. I could tell from across the room that you have a gift."

Anika raised an eyebrow. "An *artist*?"

"Yeah," he said, smiling. "I mostly work with oil paint. Abstract stuff. Not as expressive as what you're doing here, though."

She felt a small spark of curiosity. "What kind of abstract work?"

John's face lit up. "Shapes, textures, and layers. I enjoy creating things that evoke emotions in people, even if they can't put it into words. Kind of like what you're doing with your sketches."

For the first time in weeks, Anika felt a glimmer of connection. She didn't say much but listened as John talked about his art. His voice was soothing, and he didn't press her to share more than she was comfortable with. They talked for a while longer until, eventually, John finished his coffee and stood up.

"Well, looks like I'm due for a refill. I'll let you get back to it," John said, smiling. "But if you ever want to talk more about art–or anything– I'm usually around here in the evenings. This café is a great place to unwind."

Anika nodded, watching as he went towards the café counter. She wasn't sure how to feel about the encounter, but it was nice to engage with like-minded company. She opened her sketchbook again, her pencil moving across the page with a little less heaviness than before. Yet within seconds, Anika's hand paused over her sketchbook as a flood of memories washed over her. The café, with its warm, calm ambiance, suddenly felt like a glass bubble threatening to crack under the weight of her thoughts. It was clear that she was still recovering from the trauma she had endured; Anika was still learning how to navigate the pain.

Across the room, John got his refill and sat back in his original seat. Looking back at Anika, he easily sensed her distraction. Getting her attention, he broke the silence. "You okay?" he mouthed gently from across the room, his tone soft but curious.

Anika blinked, realizing she'd been staring at the same spot on her paper for too long. "Yeah, just lost in thought," she murmured, her voice betraying her exhaustion.

"Understandable," he said, getting up and reclaiming his seat next to her. "Art has a way of getting us tangled up in our own heads."

She looked at him more closely this time. His features were striking but softened by his calm demeanor. The wolf print on his shirt seemed almost symbolic—a lone wolf, free but solitary.

"You said you paint?" she asked, her voice quieter now but laced with curiosity.

"Yeah," John said with a nod. "Mostly abstract stuff. I like to build things out of chaos."

"*Chaos*," she echoed, her gaze returning to her drawing. Anika knew all about chaos. She had spent the last few months trying to make sense of it and turn it into something meaningful.

"Do you ever feel like your art is the only thing that gets you?" he asked suddenly.

She froze, her pencil hovering above the page. The question was so precise and raw that she didn't know how to answer. She nodded slowly.

"Yeah," John said, offering a small, knowing smile. "Me too."

Just then, Anika felt a strange connection to John. He wasn't prying or judging–just understanding. It was both unsettling and comforting at the same time. She smiled at him, understandingly.

Around them, the café's dim lighting softened the edges of the world. For a brief moment, Anika allowed herself to exist in this quiet space, where art and unspoken understanding had brought the two strangers together. Though there were one or two other customers present, it felt like they were the only two people present.

Anika hesitated for a moment, her fingers tracing the edges of her closed sketchbook. It had been a while since anyone asked her that question without an ulterior motive or judgment. "I really enjoy drawing," she said finally, her voice soft. "I used to do it when I was younger, but now, it's the only thing that feels real to me sometimes. Like, I can let everything out without saying a word."

John nodded thoughtfully. "I get that. Art speaks when words fail. It's why I teach–helping others find their voice through painting."

She glanced at him, intrigued. "How did *you* get into teaching?"

He smiled faintly, leaning back in his chair. "It wasn't planned, honestly. I started painting as a kid–grew up in a chaotic household, so it was my escape. Over time, it became my language, my way of making sense of everything. Eventually, I realized I wanted to share that with others, especially those who don't have a voice."

Anika studied him, sensing a genuine passion behind his words. "That's...admirable. Teaching can't be easy."

"It's not," he admitted, chuckling lightly. "But it's rewarding. Watching someone create something personal and unique–it's like witnessing a piece of their soul come alive on the canvas."

They sat in silence for a moment, the quiet hum of the café filling the space between them. "What about you?" he asked, breaking the silence. "What do you want to do with your art?"

The question hit her harder than she expected. What *did* she want? She had spent so much time surviving that dreams and ambitions felt like luxuries she couldn't afford. "I don't know," she admitted, her voice barely above a whisper. "I haven't thought that far ahead."

He tilted his head, his gaze kind but persistent. "Maybe you should. Your work deserves to be seen. And maybe, just *maybe*, it could help you heal."

Anika looked down at her sketchbook, his words lingering in her mind. *Could her art be more than just an outlet? Could it be a way to rebuild herself?* "Maybe," she said quietly, the faintest glimmer of hope flickering in her chest.

The First Step

The next morning, Anika got up and made herself a cup of tea, her hands trembling slightly. As she sipped the warm liquid, she couldn't help but replay John's words at the café: *"If you have a vision, life will make more sense to you."*

Anika sat at her small kitchen table, her sketchbook in front of her. She flipped through the pages, each one filled with drawings that carried fragments of her emotions, experiences, and pain. But now, she began to see them in a different light. What if her art wasn't just an outlet but a way to discover this "vision" John had spoken about?

Out of curiosity, Anika searched for the business card John had given her the day before. She found it effortlessly in her bag and began to examine it. The card was simple, with his name, **"John Carter,"** printed in clean, bold letters, along with the name of the community center and a phone number. She hesitated for a moment, unsure whether she should reach out regarding the art class he had mentioned teaching.

After a few minutes of internal debate, Anika decided to send a text:

"Hi, John. This is Anika from the café. I've been thinking about what you said yesterday. I'd like to understand more about vision and how art can inspire others."

She stared at her phone, nervous about what his response would be. A few minutes later, her phone buzzed. It was a message from John:

"Hi, Anika! Great to hear from you. I'm glad you're interested. I have a free afternoon tomorrow. Would you like to meet at the community center around 4 pm? I can show you around and we can talk more."

Anika hesitated but finally typed back: *"Okay. I'll be there."*

After the text exchange, Anika felt a spark of hope. She didn't know if this was the beginning of something meaningful, but it was a step forward for now.

* * *

The next day, Anika woke up early and excitedly began to prepare herself for her meeting with John. When she arrived at the community center, she stepped into the room, feeling both nervous and curious. The art class was lively, with easels arranged in a semi-circle and a group of people of various ages already working on their canvases. The atmosphere felt warm and inviting.

"Everyone, this is Anika," John announced to the class. "She's a talented artist who's here to join us today. Anika, grab a canvas and some paints from the back."

Anika quickly waved at the group and nodded at John. She made her way to the supply table. She hesitated for a moment, unsure if she belonged here, but took a deep breath and selected a blank canvas, some brushes, and paints.

As she set up her station, John walked over to her. "Today, we're working on a theme: *'What does freedom look like to you?'* Think about what freedom means to you personally and express it on the canvas. Don't overthink it–just let it flow."

Anika stared at her blank canvas. *Freedom.* The word felt distant to her. Her life had been anything but free; she had been trapped in cycles of poor choices, shame, and regret. She closed her eyes for a moment, letting the word sink in. Then, she began to paint, her brush moving instinctively across the canvas. She painted dark woods at first, with twisting trees that seemed to close in on her. Then, in the center of the painting, she added a faint golden light breaking through the forest–a path leading out of the darkness.

As the class went on, she noticed John moving around, offering guidance to the other students. When he finally came to her, he stood silently for a moment, observing her work.

"This is powerful," he said. "The contrast between the darkness and the light speaks of transformation, of finding a way out. Tell me, what does this light mean to you?"

Anika looked at the painting, her emotions bubbling to the surface. "I don't know...maybe it's hope? Or maybe, it's the vision you talked about."

John smiled gently. "A vision isn't something you just *find*. It's something you create. It's the clarity to see where you want to go and the courage to take steps. It seems like you're already starting to discover yours."

John's words struck a chord with her. She felt a flicker of purpose. Maybe Anika didn't have all the answers yet, but she realized she didn't need to. Her journey was beginning, and for the first time, she was ready to take the first step.

After some time had passed, the class came to a close. As Anika gathered her things, John handed her a flyer. "We're hosting an art exhibit next month, showcasing work from this class. I think you should submit something. Your art has a story to tell."

Anika nodded in agreement, holding the flyer tightly. As she left the community center, she felt a sense of relief. She wasn't entirely sure what the future held, but she knew she didn't have to face it alone. And maybe, just maybe, she was finally on the path to finding her vision.

New Beginnings

Anika stepped out of her apartment into the crisp October evening. The rain had picked up since earlier, now falling steadily in a misty sheet that made the cold bite deeper. She tucked her chin into her scarf and pulled her jacket tighter around her, wishing she'd remembered to grab an umbrella. The streets glistened under the streetlights, their reflections rippling in puddles as cars splashed by. Anika hurried along the sidewalk, her shoes splashing through shallow pools of water. Despite the chill, her mind was ablaze. Her thoughts circled the question that had haunted her since she first met John: *What is a vision?*

The Blooming Café came into view, its warm glow spilling out onto the wet pavement. She quickened her pace, the sight of the familiar space offering a small comfort. As she pushed open the door, the bell jingled softly, and the cozy warmth of the coffee shop enveloped her. The smell of sweet drinks and freshly baked pastries mingled with the hum of conversation, created an inviting atmosphere.

As Anika walked in, she noticed that John was already inside, sitting at a corner table near the window. He looked up as she entered, offering her a small wave and a smile. Anika greeted him in return, brushing raindrops from her jacket as she sat down across from him.

"Rough weather out there," John said, his voice warm and casual.

"You can say that again," Anika replied, shaking her head. "I should've brought an umbrella."

John chuckled lightly. "Montreal in October, right?"

Anika nodded in agreement.

Noticing her arrival, the waitress came over to take her order. Anika politely asked for a hot chocolate, craving its warmth. A few minutes later, when it arrived, she took a sip, savoring the comforting sweetness. Then she turned to John, her expression serious.

"Okay," she began, setting her mug down. "I've been thinking about this nonstop. You said the word 'vision,' and it's like–it's stuck in my head. I need to know what it means, and why it's affecting me like this."

John leaned back in his chair, studying her for a moment before speaking.

"Anika," he said, his tone gentle but deliberate, "a vision isn't just a goal or an idea. It's deeper than that. It's a picture of what you want your life to stand for. It's the thing that gives you direction and purpose. Without it, we can feel lost, like we're wandering."

Anika frowned slightly, wrapping her hands around her mug. "But how do you *find* it? I feel like I've been lost for so long. I don't even know where to start."

John nodded. "That's normal. Finding your vision isn't something that happens overnight. It's a process of self-discovery. You start by asking yourself questions: *What do you care about deeply? What makes you feel alive? What kind of impact do you want to have on the world?*"

She hesitated, the weight of his words settling over her. "I don't know if I have answers to those questions. I've spent so much time running from my past, trying to survive; I don't even know who I am anymore."

John leaned forward, his eyes kind but serious. "Then maybe this is the time to start finding out. You've already taken a step by showing up tonight and asking these questions. You're looking for something more, and that's the first step toward finding it."

Anika was quiet for a moment, her mind racing. She thought of her sketches, drawings, and how she poured her emotions onto paper. Maybe there was something there–something that could guide her toward understanding herself better.

"Do you think art could help?" she asked hesitantly.

John smiled. "Absolutely. Art is one of the most powerful tools for self-expression and discovery. It lets you explore your thoughts and emotions in ways that words sometimes can't. Keep drawing, painting– whatever feels right. Use it to reflect on what matters to you. And don't rush the process. Your vision will come into focus when the time is right."

Anika nodded slowly, her grip on her mug tightening. She was beginning to feel more hopeful for her future, so maybe she could find her way out of the darkness, too.

"Thank you," she said softly.

John nodded, his smile reassuring. "You're welcome. And remember, you're not alone in this. I'm here if you need guidance or someone to talk to."

The rain outside continued to fall, but inside the café, Anika felt a warmth that had nothing to do with the hot chocolate in her hands. Perhaps this was the beginning of something new—a step toward uncovering the vision that had eluded her for so long.

* * *

Later that night, Anika sat alone in her apartment. She spread her paintings across the floor. Each one seemed to tell a part of her story: the pain, the struggles, the flickers of hope she hadn't noticed before. Her eyes drifted to the painting John called a "Message of Freedom."

Before leaving the café that day, John had suggested Anika register for an upcoming art showcase. As she stood in her room, she could see her potential art on display: a glimmer of light breaking through the shadows, colors blending into something that felt like release. Maybe John was right. Maybe her story wasn't just hers to carry. Perhaps it was time for the world to see it.

By the time the sun rose the next morning, Anika had finally made her decision: she was going to participate in the event. She he wasn't entirely sure what she hoped to gain from it, but for the first time in a long time, she felt a spark of something new—hope.

The True Taste of Freedom

The morning of the event arrived faster than Anika anticipated. The soft golden light of dawn crept through her window, and she found herself wide awake before her alarm. Her nerves were on edge, her mind racing with a blend of excitement and fear.

After a quick breakfast, she carefully loaded her paintings into her bag, double-checking each one to ensure they were secure. She looked at the mirror one last time before heading out, taking a deep breath to steady herself. *"You've got this,"* she whispered, channeling John's encouragement.

The Anchor Art Museum buzzed with activity when she arrived, and the energy in the room was electric. The polished floors reflected the soft glow of crystal chandeliers, and the faint hum of classical music filled the air. Other artists were unpacking their work and arranging their canvases, sculptures, and installations in designated spaces. It made Anika feel small among the crowd of impeccably dressed individuals–their laughter and conversations buzzing around her. She gripped the edges of her portfolio, trying to steady her breathing.

"Anika!" John's voice cut through the crowd. He walked toward her with his usual warm smile, dressed sharply in a tailored suit. Anika, I'm so glad you're here," John said, his tone warm. "I've been looking forward to seeing your portfolio."

Anika gave a slight, grateful nod. She carefully pulled out her pieces in front of him, one by one. As each artwork was revealed, John's eyes widened, his breath catching in his throat.

"Wow…" he murmured, barely above a whisper. "They're absolutely stunning.

Anika was humbled. "Thank you," she said, blushing, her voice barely audible.

"Are you ready for this?" he asked, his tone encouraging.

She nodded hesitantly. "As ready as I'll ever be."

John laughed softly. "That's all you need. Come on, let's set these up."

Anika's booth was a modest space with clean white walls and a small wooden table. She took her time hanging her paintings carefully and placing small handwritten labels beneath each one. Additionally, John was alongside, helping to arrange each piece strategically to draw attention.

When Anika stepped back and looked at the display, it felt surreal to see her work in such a prestigious setting. Her heart was pounding. Seeing her paintings displayed like this—out in the open, vulnerable to judgment and admiration alike—was both terrifying and exhilarating.

As the event began, visitors trickled in and their chatter filled the air. Some strolled casually from booth to booth, while others paused to study the art. Anika stayed near her display, trying to appear approachable even as her stomach twisted with nerves. Publicly unveiling her work was a huge step. She desperately wanted this night to be successful.

Just then, a middle-aged woman wearing a stylish scarf stopped at Anika's booth. Her eyes lingered on the "Message of Freedom" painting.

"This piece is *incredible*," the woman said, turning to Anika. "The colors, the movement—it's so evocative. What inspired it?"

Anika hesitated, but then remembered John's words about sharing her story. "It's about breaking free from darkness," she said, her voice steadying. "Finding hope even when it feels impossible."

The woman nodded thoughtfully. "You've captured that beautifully. I want to place a bid on this piece."

Anika blinked, momentarily stunned. "Thank you," she managed to say, a nervous but genuine smile spreading across her face, "I would be honored!"

Over time, more people stopped by, asking questions and offering kind words about her work. Each interaction built Anika's confidence more and more. She felt a sense of pride she hadn't experienced in years.

Eventually, the event host, Mark Dillon, approached Anika's booth. "Anika Bailes, correct?" he said, extending a hand.

"Yes–that's me!" Anika said, returning his handshake.

"I've been hearing wonderful things about your work tonight," Mr. Dillon said, gesturing to the paintings. "Your pieces have a raw honesty that resonates deeply," he said, handing her a business card. "I'm a gallery owner, and I'd love to discuss the possibility of featuring your art in one of our upcoming exhibitions at the Rise Hotel."

Anika stared at the card, her heart leaping. Her breath was caught in her throat. "I, I don't know what to say! *Thank you!*" she said, her voice almost trembling.

"Say yes," Mr. Dillon said with a grin. "You have a unique voice; the world deserves to hear it."

Anika nodded excitedly and agreed to contact him the next day for more information. She had every intention of taking him up on this once-in-a-lifetime opportunity. It was a dream come true!

As the art showcase came to an end, she found herself standing beside John. Hopeful for her future, Anika watched as the museum staff carefully packed up her paintings.

"*You did it,*" John said, his voice filled with pride.

"I did," Anika replied, a mix of disbelief and joy washing over her.

"And this is just the beginning," John added.

After the event, Anika felt a profound shift within herself. She had taken a leap, faced her fears, and found not only validation but a glimmer of a new path forward. For the first time in years, Anika felt a sense of purpose–a belief that her art and story could make a difference. She wasn't just surviving anymore; she was creating, dreaming, and moving forward. She was beginning to experience the authentic taste of freedom.

* * *

Heading home, Anika shared a cab with John. The hum of the engine filled the silence as she gazed out of the window at the city lights. It was a quiet ride as Anika's mind raced with the events of the evening: the applause, the bids, the incredible job offer from Mark Dillon, and most of all, the overwhelming sense of validation.

As the cab pulled up to her apartment building, she turned to John to offer one last word of gratitude. Her heart was full of thanksgiving. "I mean it, John. *Thank you.* You believed in me when I couldn't believe in myself. Tonight wouldn't have happened without you."

John smiled, his expression gentle but proud. "Anika, all I did was open a door. You're the one who walked through it. And look at what you've accomplished! This is the start of something new.."

She felt a lump in her throat but managed to keep her composure. Humbled, she replied, "Still, you've been like...a guide. You saw something in me when I couldn't see it myself."

"That's what friends do," John said. "They help you see the light when all you can see is the dark."

Anika nodded, her eyes glistening. "I don't know how I'll ever repay you."

John chuckled. "You don't need to. Just keep going. Keep believing in yourself and your art. That's all the thanks I need."

She leaned over and hugged him tightly. "I will. I promise."

Relinquishing the embrace, Anika reached for the door handle and got out of the car. She closed the door behind her, stepping back to give one last wave to John. As the cab drove off, she remained standing at the entrance of her building. Anika took a deep breath. She felt a spark of hope—not just in her art but in herself.

Walking up the stairs to her apartment, she thought about the opportunities ahead: the job offer at the Rise Hotel, the newfound confidence in her talent, and the chance to inspire others through her work. She smiled to herself, realizing that this night had been a turning point. When she entered her apartment, she stood in the living room, looking around at the sketches and canvases that had once felt like a secret world she couldn't share.

"*Not anymore,*" she whispered to herself. Art was her new beginning, and Anika was finally ready to embrace it.

Distractions and Temptations

That night, Anika lay on her bed, staring at the ceiling. Her thoughts were a tangled web of hope and uncertainty. The warmth of John's words still lingered in her mind, his encouragement a small but steady beacon amid the chaos of her former life.

Her mind wandered back to the choices she had made—choices she wasn't proud of but had felt necessary to survive. Leaving home had been a desperate attempt to carve out her destiny, but she had lost sight of who she truly was somewhere along the way. Prostitution had been a way to make quick money, but it had also chained her to a life she no longer wanted. The persistent calls from Madam Hayes were a stark reminder of the past she was trying to leave behind. Anika sighed as she glanced at her phone, the missed calls glaring back at her. She blocked the number, her heart racing as she continued to take steps toward cutting ties with that chapter of her life.

Her thoughts shifted to the word that had surfaced in her mind earlier: **focus**. It felt like more than a word; it was a mantra, a guiding principle. She grabbed her sketchbook and began sketching a new painting concept. It depicted a person standing on a narrow path, surrounded by distractions and temptations, but their eyes were fixed on a distant, glowing horizon.

"*This is it,*" she murmured to herself. "*This is what I need to live by.*"

John's advice echoed in her mind: "*Pray for direction. Let your life find order.*"

She hadn't prayed in years, but something about the simplicity and sincerity of his suggestion resonated with her. She sat in bed, clasped her hands, and closed her eyes.

"*God,*" she whispered, trembling, "*I don't know where to start. My life's been a mess, and I've made mistakes. But if you're listening, I need Your help. Please show me the way. Help me focus on what matters and give me the strength to let go of the things that hold me back.*"

As she finished, a sense of calm washed over her. It wasn't a solution but a start—a moment of peace amid the storm.

* * *

The next morning, Anika woke up feeling lighter, as though the prayer had eased some of the weight she'd been carrying. She glanced at the clock and realized it was nearly 9 am. Remembering what had happened the night before, she quickly dialed the number Mark Dillon had given her.

"Hello, this is Mark," the voice on the other end said.

"Hello, Mr. Dillon. This is Anika Bales. I wanted to follow up on the opportunity you mentioned last night."

"Ah, Anika! Perfect timing. I was hoping to hear from you. Let's set up a meeting. I'd love to discuss how we can work together to showcase your art."

As they arranged the details, Anika felt a surge of optimism. Her life was beginning to align with her dreams. The road ahead wouldn't be easy, but she was ready to walk it with focus, faith, and determination. She was prepared to build a life she could be proud of.

A few hours later, Anika's phone started ringing. The screen displayed an unknown number. Anika hesitated before deciding to ignore it. Almost immediately, the phone rang again from the same unknown number. A sense of unease crept in. Thinking it might be some emergency, she finally answered.

"Hello?"

"Anika! It's me, Martine! Where have you been!?"

A knot formed in Anika's stomach at the sound of her voice. She realized she had to confront once again the situation she had been dreading–the tragic event that took place at the hotel with James and his partner. Her heart pounded, but she braced herself to finally speak up about what had happened.

Martine fell silent on the other end of the line, waiting for Anika to respond. After a long pause, she spoke again, her voice quiet but steady. "Anika, Madam Hayes explained the situation to me. I'm so sorry this happened to you. And I'm deeply sorry for the loss of your baby." She paused, then continued, her tone firm yet caring. "I also need to remind you–seeing clients outside the brothel can be incredibly dangerous. Especially when you're alone with strangers and have no backup if something goes wrong."

"Thank you for reaching out and for the reminders," Anika said, her tone softening. "I am doing better and healing from what happened.

However, I've moved on from this lifestyle, and I'd prefer it if you never contact me again. Thank you."

Before Martine could respond, Anika hung up the phone. She was shocked by the strength of her voice and actions. A few weeks ago, Anika never would've had the courage to speak up for herself like this. Her response was proof that she was experiencing growth in her personal development. She had her art to thank for this!

After the call, Anika turned her attention back to her supplies. Sitting at her small kitchen table, she began sketching the outline of her next painting. This one would be called *"Renewal."* She envisioned a woman standing under a waterfall, shedding layers of pain and guilt as the water washed over her; renewed and ready to face the world.

Second Thoughts

As Anika lay in bed that night, her mind replayed the conversation with Martine. Tossing and turning, she couldn't sleep. Each word they had spoken echoed in the silence like a thread pulling at something buried deep within her. Anika had no desire to return to her old life at the brothel. Yet, her nervous system remained dysregulated–tugging her back toward the familiar rush of fast money and fleeting power she once commanded.

Confusion had settled in. Was Anika longing for financial stability or the seductive chaos she'd barely escaped? Her heart wavered, but her flesh remembered. The temptation of luxurious prostitution was creeping back in. Especially because she knew she couldn't survive off of her savings forever.

Even though Madam Hayes had shut the door on her the moment she learned of Anika's tragedy, Anika held on to a fragile hope that she could still contribute to the industry. She decided she would call Martine back and tell her she was having second thoughts. After all, enough time had passed–she could always rebuild her reputation. Perhaps she could reclaim the power she had lost following that tragic incident. It looked like Martine had convinced her after all. Maybe there was a second chance waiting for her behind those velvet curtains.

CHAPTER 5
The World of Luxury

After reaching out to Martine to discuss the possibility of being rehired, Anika understood there would be rules she would have to follow. As a condition for her return to the industry, Madam Hayes advised her to avoid engaging in sex work outside the brothel, citing obvious concerns for her safety. Agreeing to the terms, Anika was nervous and excited to step back into her old lifestyle. Her next step was an in-person meeting with Martine at a new upscale brothel location in Las Vegas, Nevada.

Highly motivated to get started, Anika quickly wrapped up business at home. Within one week, she broke her lease, packed up her things, and booked the next flight out. Afraid of what Rachel, John, or Mr. Dillon might think, Anika decided not to inform them she was moving. Knowing she would owe them an explanation, she felt it would be less painful to disappear without warning. As soon as her flight landed, Anika contacted

Martine to discuss the next steps. She was told to take a cab to *Luxury World.*

Upon arriving, Anika followed Martine to her office, her heels clicked softly against the marble floor. The opulence of the establishment was overwhelming–the chandeliers, polished gold accents, and velvet furnishings screamed wealth and exclusivity. Martine's office was no different, with its sleek black desk, floor-to-ceiling windows, and a bar stocked with the finest liquors. She motioned for Anika to sit on the plush chair in front of her desk. Anika complied and sat across from her–leaning in with a mix of excitement and professionalism. Martine wasted no time getting down to business.

"Anika," she began, "let me be clear about what this place is. Luxury World isn't just a brothel–it's a *brand.* Our clients are among the wealthiest individuals globally. They're CEOs, celebrities, and diplomats. They come here expecting discretion, sophistication, and the absolute best, and *that's* what we give them."

Anika nodded silently, absorbing every word.

"Now, I know you've worked with me before, but this location has higher expectations. You're not just here to look pretty; you're here to provide an *experience.* These clients pay tens of thousands of dollars per night for our services. You'll need to be well-groomed, articulate, and adaptable. I've already scheduled an appointment for you with our stylist and etiquette coach. As you become reacquainted with the business, I want you to *shine.*"

Martine's words were smooth and convincing, but felt heavy. Anika's stomach churned as she thought about what she was stepping into.

"I also want to address safety," Martine continued. "As I mentioned previously, Luxury World has strict protocols. Security is tight, and every client is thoroughly vetted. No one enters this building without first passing a background check and undergoing a health screening. In addition to providing excellent customer service, Luxury World aims to ensure that all staff feel safe and cared for. Our in-house doctor and counselor are on call 24 hours a day, 7 days a week–if there's *anything* you need, ask and you'll receive it." Then Martine leaned back, smiling. "So, what do you think so far?"

Anika hesitated. "It's...impressive," she admitted. "You've built something extraordinary here."

"Thank you," Martine said, her grin widening. "I built this because I know how hard it is for women like us. This isn't just a business; it's an empire. I want you to be part of it."

Anika nodded, still unsure. The luxurious surroundings and Martine's persuasive words made it seem glamorous. Still, a voice in the back of her mind whispered doubts. She lacked understanding of what was in store.

"I'll give you the night to settle in," Martine said, standing up. "Your first day starts tomorrow. Take this time to explore, relax, and get a feel for the new environment. If you need anything, my assistant is just a call away. She'll give you more details on your appointment."

Nodding understandingly, Anika stood up and thanked Martine for the hospitality. Hopeful, she looked forward to seeing her new room. Maybe Luxury World wouldn't be so bad after all.

Settling In

Finally settled into her new Nevada home, Anika sat on the edge of the plush bed in her private suite, staring out at the city lights through the floor-to-ceiling window. With the door closed, the silence of the lavish room began to envelop her. The room was nothing short of breathtaking–

sleek modern furniture, a panoramic view of the city, and a plush king-sized bed adorned with silky sheets. The neutral tones of the decor were complemented by subtle gold accents, exuding an air of exclusivity and luxury.

Nevada was alive with energy, and the streets below teemed with activity. She had traveled a long way from home to be here, and the views did not disappoint. Anika should have felt excited, but instead, a deep unease settled over her. She opened her phone and scrolled through the photos she had taken earlier. The vibrant lights, the luxurious interiors–it all looked like a dream. As Anika stared at them, she realized how detached she felt from it all.

Her thoughts drifted to her life before Luxury World. Anika had made significant sacrifices to return to the world of prostitution. Just a few days prior, her paintings had brought her a sense of purpose. Now, her beloved city of Montreal, her first apartment, which she had grown to love, her developing mentorship with John, and her dream job at the Rise Hotel were all but a memory. Would her presence at Luxury World make it all worthwhile? She realized only time would tell.

Anika's mind raced. The "girlfriend experience" Martine had mentioned earlier sounded like an enticing pitch–lavish dates, control over her choices, and a hefty paycheck that could solve her financial woes. But at what cost? She thought about Martine's confidence in her, the other women she'd seen earlier, and her own past experiences.

"Is this *really* what I want?" she whispered to herself. Lying back on the bed, Anika stared at the ornate ceiling. Tomorrow would bring new challenges, and she wasn't sure if she was ready to face them. For now, she could only hope she was making the right choice. If things didn't pan out the way she envisioned, she promised herself she wouldn't hesitate to change courses.

Looking out the window again, she saw the dazzling lights of the Strip. It was a city that promised excitement, reinvention, and escape, but deep down, she knew it could also be unforgiving. She remembered Martine's words from earlier: *"Give yourself a nickname and change up your persona a bit."* What did *that* mean? Strip away *more* of herself? Wear a mask even thicker than the one she'd already been forced to put on?

Overwhelmed with emotions, Anika stood up and wandered around the room. Her thoughts became heavier with each step. She opened the wardrobe to find an array of lingerie sets, each one more delicate and provocative than the last. The sight of them made her stomach twist. This wasn't just about looking beautiful or alluring; it was about playing a role, about losing herself in someone else's fantasy.

Stuck in her thoughts, the sudden sound of her door opening snapped her back to reality. In walked one of the other escorts, a tall woman with striking features and an air of confidence.

"Hey, you're Anika, right? I'm Giselle," she said with a warm smile. "Martine asked me to check on you and help you settle in."

Anika managed a small smile. "Thanks. I'm just processing everything."

Giselle nodded knowingly. "It's a lot at first. I've been here a year, and trust me, it gets easier. You have to find your rhythm, you know? And don't stress too much about tomorrow's lineup. Most clients are regulars, and they're pretty respectful."

Anika nodded, her thoughts still swirling.

"Anyway," Giselle continued, "if you need anything, I'm just down the hall. And don't worry about the nickname thing–pick something that makes you feel powerful. This is your world now. *Own it.*"

After Giselle left, Anika sat back on the bed in silence, staring at the shimmering skyline. She was at a crossroads, caught between the promise of wealth and the weight of her conscience. Anika knew she needed to make a decision soon, but for now, all she could do was breathe and take in the moment. In this new chapter of life, she believed things would get easier if she figured out who she wanted to be.

First Day Back

As Anika sat on the couch the next day, her heart raced. The living room exuded an air of luxury, with velvet furniture and soft lighting casting an inviting glow. The other women seemed at ease, their laughter light and confident as they spoke with the client. Anika, on the other hand, felt a knot tighten in her stomach.

The client, a sharply dressed man in his late forties, seemed polite but carried an air of authority. His eyes moved from one woman to the next as he made small talk, asking questions about their interests and hobbies. When his gaze finally landed on Anika, she felt exposed, as though he could see every ounce of her hesitation.

"And what about *you?*" he asked, his voice smooth. "What's your name?"

Anika hesitated for a moment before recalling Martine's advice about a nickname. "Call me...Bella," she said, her voice steady despite the nerves coursing through her. She'd chosen the name on a whim, hoping it sounded alluring yet approachable.

"Bella," he repeated, a small smile playing on his lips. "That's a lovely name. So, Bella, tell me—what do you enjoy doing for fun?"

She paused, glancing briefly at the other women before replying. "I enjoy painting," she said, her voice soft but clear. "It's something that helps me relax and express myself."

The client raised an eyebrow, intrigued. "Interesting. Do you paint landscapes, portraits, or something else?"

"A little of everything," Anika replied, feeling slightly more at ease. "But I mostly paint portraits. There's something about capturing emotions on a canvas that I find fascinating."

Their conversation continued for a few minutes, and Anika began to feel more relaxed. She could feel the tension in her shoulders easing as she spoke about her art and answered his questions. The other women occasionally chimed in, but the client's focus remained on her.

After a while, he stood and addressed Martine, who had been watching from a distance. "I think I've made my choice," he said, his voice carrying across the room.

Martine walked over, her expression calm but expectant. "And who would you like to spend your evening with?"

"Bella," he said, his eyes meeting Anika's. "She has a certain...*charm*."

Martine smiled approvingly. "Excellent choice. Bella, please follow me."

Anika stood up, her legs feeling slightly unsteady in her heels. As she followed Martine out of the room, she couldn't help but feel a mix of emotions–relief that she'd been chosen, anxiety about what lay ahead, and a lingering sense of doubt about whether she truly belonged in this world.

Just outside the door, Martine stopped and whispered to Anika, "You did great. Just be yourself, and remember–you're in control. If anything feels wrong, come to me immediately."

Anika nodded, taking a deep breath. Looking back at her client, she forced a smile and prepared herself to step into the next chapter of this strange, complicated journey. Taking Martine's advice, she returned to her room to select her outfit for the evening. Her thoughts raced as she combed through her wardrobe options. It was her first day back in the world of prostitution, and she wanted to make a good impression. Eventually, she decided on a sleek black cocktail dress with a subtle shimmer. She paired it with matching heels and simple jewelry, aiming for elegance rather than extravagance.

Before heading out, she glanced at herself one last time in the mirror, adjusting her hair and makeup. "*This is just a night out,*" she told herself. "*Be professional. Keep it simple.*"

Her client, Greg, was waiting for her in the lounge area when she arrived. He stood as she approached, his eyes scanning her with approval. "You look stunning," he said with a warm smile.

"Thank you," Anika replied, returning his smile. She couldn't deny that his polished demeanor put her slightly at ease.

They stepped out into the fabulous Nevada night, the city lights illuminating the streets with their vibrant glow. A sleek black car awaited them, and Greg opened the door for her before getting in himself. As they drove to their destination, Anika initiated a lighthearted conversation. Appreciative, Greg engaged and complimented her on how well she listened. The night was off to a great start.

When they arrived at the bar on Dexter Street, Anika could not hide her expression. She was highly impressed by the relaxed yet upscale vibe. It was quieter than the bustling casinos, and the low hum of conversation and jazz music filled the air. Greg led them to a cozy corner table, where a server promptly greeted them.

Eventually, they began to chat over cocktails. Greg was charming, effortlessly weaving stories about his work and travels into the conversation. At one point, he casually mentioned that he was a married man. In this line of work, Anika wasn't surprised anymore. She listened attentively, occasionally sharing anecdotes of her own, careful to keep things light and impersonal. She found herself enjoying the conversation more than she'd anticipated. Yet, she remained conscious of the line between her role and personal feelings.

As the evening progressed, Greg leaned back in his chair, studying her. "You're *different*," he said thoughtfully. "Not like the others."

"How so?" Anika asked, keeping her tone casual.

"You seem...grounded. Like you're here because you've *chosen* to be, not because you *have* to be."

Anika smiled faintly, unsure how to respond. She sipped her drink, choosing her words carefully before putting it back down. "I believe in making the best of any situation. Life is about choices, and I try to approach everything with a positive mindset."

Greg nodded, seeming satisfied with her answer. "That's a good philosophy."

* * *

As the night continued, Anika and Greg left the bar and rode back home together in the familiar black car. The night air was crisp, and the streets were quieter than before. When they arrived back at the brothel, Greg got out of the vehicle and escorted Anika back to the front door. His demeanor was respectful, and his eyes were kind.

As they stood outside her new home, it finally appeared to Anika that Greg was ending the night early. In shock, Anika stood there–she couldn't believe the date was almost over and Greg hadn't initiated any physical contact. As they exchanged goodbye pleasantries, Greg reached towards his pocket and pulled out an envelope. Much to Anika's surprise, she opened it and found a generous tip inside. Looking back up at Greg with wide eyes, Anika didn't know what to say.

Internally, gratitude was what Greg's heart had been lacking. His appointment with Anika was unlike any other he had experienced with a sex worker. Through a thoughtful and genuine conversation, she seemed to pinpoint the root of Greg's unrest. Truth be told, he had started visiting Luxury World after an ongoing conflict with his wife. All along, he thought he was seeking the comfort of physical intimacy. But what he discovered instead–with Anika's insight–was that he truly yearned for a deeper understanding of appreciation. In that unexpected moment, Greg began to realize that what he truly needed was to learn how to appreciate the woman he had almost lost.

Noticing Anika's surprise as she glanced at the amount written on the check, Greg let out a soft, knowing laugh. "Love is about giving," he said gently. "It's how we show gratitude. Thank you for tonight, Anika. Talking with you–it was truly a gift."

With that, he turned and walked toward his car, leaving Anika standing in quiet disbelief, the check still trembling slightly in her hand.

"So, Greg tipped me…with NO sexual interaction!?" she thought to herself. She was genuinely confused and relieved at the same time. Finally finding the words to speak, she called out to him just as he was grabbing the door handle.

"Wait! I'm sorry, I'm just speechless. Thank you for the tip Greg. Honestly, the pleasure was all mine," she said, smiling appreciatively.

Stopping to look back at her, Greg returned a smile.

"Could you…Could you wait here, Greg?" Anika continued, "I have something for you. Could you please give me ten minutes? I promise it will be worth your time."

Greg nodded and agreed to wait. Even though he didn't understand what was going on, he knew this moment mattered to Anika. Whatever it was she had in store for him was worth waiting for.

Determined not to let the moment slip away, Anika returned to her room and gathered her painting supplies. It was the one thing she had brought from Montreal that reminded her of home and the normalcy that once was. She quickly set up her small workstation with quiet purpose, then pulled out a tiny canvas. Her brush moved almost instinctively–each stroke flowing like a gentle stream, guided not by thought, but by feelings. The colors bloomed with emotion, echoing the hope and warmth Greg's gift had stirred within her.

As the image slowly emerged, she felt something shift inside–a sense of freedom. Painting wasn't just a way to pass the time. She was painting to remember who she was, to nurture the light she'd seen reflected in Greg's eyes. And maybe, just maybe, to offer that light to someone else.

By the time she finished, her canvas revealed a vivid scene. Blooming roses emerged–encircling a heart–their petals unfurling like open arms. It was a quiet echo of what Greg had told her: *love is about giving*. She took a step back and marveled at its beauty. Anika was sure that Greg would be pleased.

Rushing back outside, she found Greg waiting exactly where she had left him. When they locked eyes, she reached out and gently handed him the painting. "This is for you," she said. "Let it dry for five to ten minutes. It's acrylic–so it shouldn't take too long."

Gazing at the art in awe, Greg accepted it with a warm smile. "Thank you," he said. "This is incredible." Then, with a playful glance over Anika's shoulder, he added, "Well, I guess it's time for me to go. You should probably head back inside, too–Martine's staring at us."

Realizing she was being watched, Anika nodded in agreement and gave Greg a quick wave goodbye. Stepping back into the brothel, she immediately noticed Martine.

"**Anika**," she said sternly, with her eyebrows raised, "why did you go back to your room only to come out again and meet your client outside? I saw you give him something–what was *that* about?"

Noticing her analyzing tone, Anika understood that she was being interrogated. She responded, "When I realized Greg wasn't interested in anything physical, I was inspired to give him a gift. The depth of our conversation truly moved him. I was returning the favor."

Martine rolled her eyes, "That's not how this business works. You're not paid to make assumptions about what you think your client wants. It's about giving them what they *pay* for."

Feeling the need to defend herself, Anika spoke up. "I understand, Martine, but he left me a generous tip. I had to give him *something* in return."

Taken aback by this news, Martine paused before responding. Throughout her time managing the business, she had never seen a client offer a tip without a sexual exchange. The encounter was a rare and uncommon exception. Nevertheless, there were rules associated with Luxury World, and it was her job to ensure Anika complied with them.

Finally speaking up, she said, "So, you're telling me that Greg gave you a tip just for a *conversation*, Anika? That is absurd. Let me make something obvious–our policy here is straightforward. Clients pay for sex. A quick chat is only meant to *lead* to that–not *replace* it. **DO NOT** make a habit of this, Anika. I'm warning you."

Anika met Martine's gaze, her voice calm but resolute. She couldn't understand why Martine was so upset. Perhaps if she could explain what happened more clearly, Martine would see her point of view.

Anika continued, "This tip was about more than money–it was the validation I didn't know I needed. It was a reminder that even in a place like Luxury World, I can still leave a lasting impact. A positive mark."

Realizing that Anika would not back down, Martine said nothing more. She gave Anika a final look, then turned and stormed off disapprovingly. The conversation remained behind her.

* * *

Left standing there alone, Anika decided to go back to her room. Inside, she found her painting supplies waiting just where she had left them. As her eyes settled on one of her completed pieces–a painted heart– she found herself filled with gratitude and renewal. The heart was a reminder that her words made a difference. More than just a decoration, the heart was a symbol of change. Picking up the small canvas, Anika set it up on her desk, positioning it where it would catch the light. She wanted it to be a constant inspiration that, despite her circumstances, she could still create beauty and encourage others.

Anika sighed deeply, feeling a mixture of pride and sadness. She was proud of what she'd accomplished with Greg, but she also couldn't ignore the uneasy tension with Martine. Would she face consequences for not fulfilling her "job" as expected? Martine's cold shoulder made Anika feel unstable about her future with Luxury World.

Though Martine's words echoed in her mind, Anika didn't regret what she had done. Consumed with her thoughts, Anika was startled when a sealed envelope suddenly slid under her door.

"Anika, it's me, Martine," she called out from the hallway. "This envelope is from your client, Greg. He left it at the front desk for you. It might be another check or something else. I don't know–I didn't open it. Anyways, he said it was for you."

Without a word, Anika quickly grabbed the envelope and opened it up. Inside was a handwritten letter.

Dear Anika,

I'm beginning to understand that genuine gratitude means appreciating what I already have—especially my wife. Because of this, I've decided I won't be returning to Luxury World. Instead, I'm going to seek therapy and put in the work my marriage deserves. Thank you for the painting. It spoke to me in a way I can't fully explain. Goodbye, Anika. I wish you well.

With gratitude,

Greg

Though Anika had lost a client, she felt a quiet sense of gratitude. She had helped Greg find his way back to his marriage, and *that* was worth more than any payment could have been.

* * *

The next morning, another knock on the door pulled Anika from her reverie. Rising from her slumber, she opened it to find Martine, who handed her the following list of appointments. Anika didn't want to admit the envelope from last night had contained a letter—not another tip—so she thanked Martine with a polite nod. Her mind was still hazy. Greg's heartfelt gesture lingered in her thoughts, a stark contrast to the reality of her work waiting just beyond the door.

"Thank you, Martine. I'll be ready," Anika said evenly, keeping her tone neutral. As she closed the door behind her, she took a steadying breath and glanced at the list: six appointments lined up, starting in just one hour. "*It's showtime,*" she murmured dispassionately to herself.

Tucking Greg's note safely in her purse, Anika started preparing for her day. The note was a small treasure she couldn't afford to lose, and she didn't want to take any chances of it being found in her room. Keeping it with her at all times was the only way to ensure its safety.

As she began to get ready, Anika reflected on how much her perspective had shifted since her arrival at Luxury World. Greg's gratitude had reignited a spark within her–a reminder of who she was before this life. She didn't want to forget that feeling, no matter how busy or overwhelming the day ahead seemed.

As she meticulously applied her makeup, styled her hair, and slipped into an elegant dress accompanied by matching high heels, something felt different. Each movement was mechanical, a well-practiced routine–yet today, it was accompanied by a quiet determination. *"This week could be more than just about making money,"* she thought as she looked in the mirror. Perhaps it could be about finding little moments of meaning–whether through art, kindness, or something unexpected.

A Different Approach

Sitting on the bed, Anika had mixed emotions. On one hand, the thought of a busy day felt exhausting, but on the other hand, the prospect of high weekly earnings was motivating. By the time her client arrived, Anika had compartmentalised her emotions. Entirely composed, she was ready to face the day. Opening the door to greet him, she showed off a practiced smile. Inspiration from Greg propelled her forward.

Today, Anika's client, Curtis, had chosen a spa for their date. It was a short commute to their destination, but Anika did her best to get to know him. Curtis was a professional football player who visited the spa regularly to unwind after the pressure and intensity of his games. She quickly learned this location was one of his favorites.

When they arrived, they wasted no time getting into the private jacuzzi. The quiet intimacy put them at ease as they soaked into the warm, bubbling water. Looking over at Curtis, a familiar client to the *Luxury World,* Anika recognized he was relaxed but slightly guarded. His tall, imposing frame contrasted with a composed calm that intrigued her–there was something grounded about him, something steady.

Analyzing his features, Anika was soon interrupted by a waitress who offered them champagne. Nodding in agreement, Curtis and Anika welcomed them cheerfully. With glasses in hand, they clinked them together playfully–a soft chime filling the air. They smiled at each other, comforted by the other's presence. Eventually, conversation began to unfold, slow and tentative, like the steam curling around them.

"So, Curtis, how's football treating you?" Anika asked, her voice smooth and conversational.

"It's good," he replied, taking a sip of his drink. "Tough season, though. Lots of pressure to perform, you know? Fans expect nothing but wins."

"I can imagine," Anika said. "All eyes on you, every move analyzed. That must be exhausting."

He nodded, his expression softening. "Yeah, it is. Don't get me wrong–I love the game. It's my passion. But sometimes, it feels like there's no room for mistakes. And when you're under that spotlight, it's hard to know who's genuinely in your corner."

"That sounds heavy," Anika said empathetically. "Do you have people you can talk to about it? Friends or family?"

Curtis chuckled lightly. "Not really. Most people want to hang out with 'Curtis Johnson, the footballer,' not the real me. It's hard to trust anyone when you're in my position."

Anika nodded, understanding more than she let on. "I get that. Sometimes, you want to be seen for who you are, not for what you do."

Curtis looked at her, a hint of surprise in his eyes. "Yeah, exactly. It's like you're speaking my mind."

Anika smiled. It felt good to build a connection with him.

They sat in silence for a moment, letting the soothing heat of the jacuzzi and the faint bubbles fill the space. Finally, Curtis broke the quiet.

"So, how about *you*? Do you like what you do here?"

Anika hesitated for a moment but decided to give a measured response. "It has its moments. It's not always about the work–it's about the connections you make, even if they're brief. Sometimes, those moments mean more than you'd think."

Curtis seemed to ponder her words, then smiled. He appreciated Anika's raw dialogue. "I didn't expect this. Thought it'd just be, well, you know, a *service*. But this? This feels real."

Anika smiled back, feeling a sense of satisfaction in the exchange. It reminded her that even in the most unlikely situations, meaningful conversations could unfold.

"Well, Curtis," she said, raising her glass, "here's to taking a break from all the pressure and just being yourself, even if it's only for three hours."

Reaching over, he clinked his glass against hers once more–a genuine grin spreading across his face. "I'll drink to *that*."

As the conversation continued, the atmosphere in the jacuzzi grew more relaxed. Curtis leaned back, letting the warm water soothe him, while Anika maintained her professional yet approachable demeanor.

Reflecting on her earlier words, Curtis decided to continue the topic. "You know, I really agree with your perspective on life," Curtis said, his tone shifting to one of genuine admiration. "It's like, you've got beauty and brains. This energy about you goes beyond your outward appearance. It's *different*. Makes a guy feel like he can actually talk to you, you know?"

Anika smiled, taking another sip of her champagne. "Thank you. I believe it's essential to create a space where people feel at ease. Whether it's for a conversation or something more, everyone deserves to feel valued."

Curtis nodded thoughtfully. "I don't think most people in my world think about things like that. It's always about the next game, the next win. No one stops to exist for a moment."

"Well, maybe that's what you needed today," Anika said, her tone gentle. "A moment to pause, let go of all that pressure, and just be present."

He chuckled, shaking his head. "You're something else, Anika. I expected this to be, well, *transactional*. However, as I mentioned earlier, it feels different. Like, you actually care."

"I do," Anika said simply. "I believe that every interaction, no matter how brief, has the potential to leave a mark. So, why not make it a good one?"

Curtis tilted his head, studying her for a moment. "You've got a way with words. Makes me wonder what you'd be doing if you weren't here."

Anika hesitated, her smile faltering just slightly. "Maybe something similar, in a way. I like connecting with people. Maybe I'd be a teacher or an artist, something where I can inspire or help others."

"I could see that," Curtis said, nodding. "You've got that vibe. You make people feel seen."

As Anika prepared to respond, their conversation was interrupted by the soft chime of the clock on the wall. Curtis glanced at it and sighed. "Guess our time's almost up. Practice calls."

Anika smiled warmly. "Well, I hope you got what you came here for—some peace, maybe even a little clarity."

"I definitely did," Curtis said, his tone sincere. "Thanks, Anika. You're good at what you do, and not just in the way people think."

As he climbed out of the jacuzzi and began to dry off, Anika felt a quiet sense of fulfillment. She had managed to end yet another date without fulfilling any sexual expectations. Moments like this reminded her why she did what she did—not just for the paycheck, but for the chance to connect, even if only briefly, with the people who walked through her door.

* * *

Overall, moving to Nevada had been a bold decision—especially returning to sex work at a legal brothel. The longer she stayed, the more she realized her desires had shifted. Over the next few weeks, she found herself reaching into the hearts of her clients rather than engaging in physical encounters. Her time at *Luxury* had already been transformative, both emotionally and financially. Yet, the success felt fleeting. As she continued to cross professional lines and break protocols, she was reminded that this chapter, however impactful, might not last.

A Dangerous Encounter

After her date, Anika returned to the brothel. Her mind was already shifting gears as she prepared for the next client on her appointment list. She moved quickly, heading to the shower to wash off the lingering scent of chlorine from the jacuzzi. After drying off, she dressed with professional precision, slipping into the persona she knew the day would demand. This time, the name on the list was Georgios Vandero.

As she stepped out of her room and walked toward the lobby, she spotted him immediately. He stood facing the window, back straight, arms crossed behind his back, and demeanor distant. It was like he owned the space without needing to say a word. When he slowly turned around, Georgios deliberately locked eyes with her.

"You must be *Anika*," he said, greasily. "I booked an appointment to meet you. I'm Georgios–but most people call me *Mr. Snake*." He tilted his head slightly, revealing the coiled red tattoo slithering up the left side of his neck.

Anika's pulse quickened. She had heard this name before. Mr. Snake was the infamous pimp that the guest speaker from her school had warned her classmates about. His reputation preceded him: dangerous and manipulative. Mr. Snake was a man known for exploiting and controlling women with terrifying efficiency. And yet here he was, standing before her with a calm smile, as if their meeting had been fated all along. The encounter was certainly not a coincidence.

Anika knew the stakes. Refusing a client could lead to trouble, especially if that client had connections or influence. But something about this situation felt different, heavier. She couldn't ignore the unease that settled in her chest.

She forced a polite smile, trying to buy herself some time. "Mr. Snake, it is a pleasure to meet you. Please follow me to your suite and allow me to help you get settled."

Pleased by her professionalism, he complied.

When they arrived, Anika opened the door and went inside. She invited Mr. Snake to follow suit. He walked in and quickly scanned the space. His body language made it clear he had impure motives. Closing the door behind him, Anika's mind raced. She made a direct path towards the bar and offered him a drink. It was a desperate attempt to keep the conversation neutral before he could find the bedroom.

"I must admit, I was surprised to see you at the door. I heard stories about you when I lived in Montreal, Canada," Anika said, handing him a glass. Her tone was steady but cautious. "So, what brings you here today?"

Georgios chuckled, his tone dripping with arrogance. He had found a seat on the couch, but his eyes were locked on Anika's frame. Taking a sip from his drink, he said, "Curiosity, mostly. I've heard a lot about you, too, Anika. You have quite a reputation–not just for your looks, but for your unique approach with clients. I wanted to see for myself."

Anika felt a chill run down her spine. She kept her composure, refusing to show any sign of fear. Resting herself against the adjacent table, she responded, "Well, I do my best to ensure every client has a good experience."

He leaned back on the couch, his gaze sharp and calculating. "That's what I like about you. You're different. But let's not waste time. I paid for a service, and I expect to receive it."

Anika hesitated, her hands gripping the edge of the table. She knew she had to make a decision–and quickly. Either she went along with his expectations and risked being entangled in whatever agenda he had, or she refused and potentially faced the consequences of defying him. Her options were clearly limited.

Taking a deep breath, she spoke firmly, her voice unwavering. She refused to be aggressively taken advantage of–not this time. "Mr. Snake, allow me to make myself **very** clear. I understand you've come here for a service, but I have certain boundaries that I must adhere to. If there's anything you expect that goes beyond what's agreed upon, I'll have to decline."

Georgios's expression darkened slightly, but then he smirked as if amused by her defiance. "*Boundaries*? That's an interesting word coming from someone in your line of work."

Anika held his gaze. "*Respect* is part of this work, Mr. Snake, and it goes both ways. If that's not something you're willing to offer me, I'm afraid this won't work. If you don't want me to contact security, feel free to let yourself out."

For a moment, the room fell silent. Georgios's smirk faded, replaced by a thoughtful expression. No one had ever spoken to him like this before. Anika's boldness had not only taken him off guard, but it also made him rethink his motives. Contemplating his next move, he finally stood and adjusted his jacket.

"You know what, Anika? You've got guts. I'll give you that," he said, his tone a mix of admiration and menace. "But remember—guts only get you so far in this world." As he walked toward the door, he paused and looked back at her. "I'll see you again soon. *Count on it.*"

When the door closed behind him, Anika let out a shaky breath and relaxed against the coffee table. It was her first dangerous encounter at Luxury World, but she won the battle against Mr. Snake by standing her ground. As much as she wanted to celebrate the small victory, Anika knew now wasn't the time. Assuming Mr. Snake would decline payment, eventually, Martine would learn what had happened and question Anika's professionalism. She knew she'd have to prepare herself to answer for her actions.

Yet, still, Anika remained hopeful. Despite what the future held, she felt good about the developmental progress she was making. Regardless of how Martine would respond, one thing was sure: Anika had found her voice and would no longer be silenced.

CHAPTER 6

The Crown She Didn't Know She Wore

Friday morning brought Anika a rare sense of calm. It was her day off, and the weight of the week's work lifted slightly as she woke up in her quiet room. She didn't have to meet clients, put on makeup, or deal with the pressures of Luxury World today. Nearby, Anika's easel stood in the corner of her room, waiting for her. She had purchased a variety of painting supplies earlier in the week. Finally, she had the chance to immerse herself in the world of colors and creativity.

Her mind was brimming with images–snippets of her life. Emotions she couldn't put into words, and the faces of people she had encountered. With each stroke of her brush, she poured her thoughts onto the canvas. The first painting was a vibrant swirl of reds and yellows, expressing the passion and chaos of her work. The second was a tranquil blend of blues and whites, a stark contrast to the first—an image of the peace she yearned for.

For her next piece, Anika began by sketching the delicate outline of a crown. She wasn't just painting for beauty this time. She wanted this work to speak to something more profound. The crown, bold yet graceful, was a symbol of how far she had come—a quiet declaration that she was worthy, valuable, and no longer afraid to take up space.

Sitting cross-legged on the room floor, Anika allowed the sunlight to filter through the dusty windowpanes and warm the tops of her hands. Around her, the scattered remnants of past projects lay in organized chaos—brushes, old canvases, sketches half-finished and once-abandoned. Yet, this piece felt different. More intentional. More personal.

After dipping her brush into a deep gold hue, she paused. The metallic pigment shimmered in the light, like a possibility made tangible. *"I'm not painting what I want to be,"* she thought. *"I'm painting what I already am—even if I'm still learning to believe it."*

As she continued, each stroke of paint felt like a reclamation. The jewels in the crown weren't just decorations—they were memories. The jewels represented the times she spoke up even though her voice shook; the days she kept going when no one noticed; and the quiet courage it took to believe she mattered. She didn't need anyone else to see the value in the crown. She saw it now. And that was enough.

* * *

As the day went on, Anika continued painting, allowing her thoughts to drift. She reflected on her time at Luxury World and the relationships she had built there. Recently, Anika had crossed paths with a girl named Mishka. It was nice to have made a friend, and she grew fond of the young woman's sweet demeanor. However, as an easily likeable colleague, Mishka was painfully trusting, and naive. Though some considered her a potential target of abuse, Anika remained hopeful for her future.

With every brush stroke, Anika's thoughts of Mishka grew more and more intense. She couldn't help but think about what had happened the previous night. Ever since Anika had witnessed Mishka volunteer to take Georgios as her client, Anika had grown concerned about her well-being. She had admired Mishka's courage–or recklessness–but hadn't seen her since they parted ways. Either way, Anika was grateful she had stood her ground against him. She didn't want to chance Georgios becoming confrontational with her, and could only hope Mishka was okay.

Losing herself in the rhythm of her work, Anika continued painting. It was as if each brushstroke healed a part of her that the demands of her job had worn down. For once, she wasn't a sex worker or a service provider. She was simply Anika–a blooming woman.

* * *

By mid-afternoon, Anika's hands were speckled with paint, and her room smelled faintly of turpentine. Finally, her thoughts had calmed. Looking around at the row of finished canvases leaning against the wall, she felt a sense of satisfaction. Each painting was a piece of her, a reminder of her resilience and creativity. This day off was exactly what she needed–a chance to reconnect with herself and regain the strength to face whatever came next.

After tidying up her workspace, Anika was startled by shouts and emotional voices echoing from the lobby. Curious and concerned, she opened her door to find several workers in tears and Martine standing nearby with her hands covering her face. Anika's heart sank–something was clearly wrong. Without hesitation, she stepped out to find out what had happened.

"At the hospital? Since *last night?*" Madam Martine asked the receptionist, her voice edged with concern. "Do you know what happened?"

Martine had been away from the building–she'd taken the day off and hadn't returned until later that morning. It was only then that she learned about Mishka's condition.

The receptionist hesitated, glancing around nervously. "Yes, since last night when Mr. Snake left the building. Not long after that, Mishka came crawling out of her room–bruised all over. It wasn't good. I called the police right away and they took her to the hospital."

Anika felt a chill crawl down her spine. Her mind flashed back to Georgios–or instead, *Mr. Snake.* She had known that refusing him had been the right decision, but now, her deepest fears were being confirmed. Georgios had chosen Mishka as his next victim.

When Martine noticed Anika, she rushed over and grabbed her hand with urgency. Recalling Anika's connection with Mr. Snake, she said, "Anika, do you know anything else about this client–Georgios? He was the last person seen with Mishka. The receptionist overheard your conversation with him the other day and mentioned the way you spoke to him. She said it seemed like you may have known him personally. Can you tell me more about this guy?"

Put on the spot, Anika hesitated. The words caught in her throat, heavy and bitter. "Well…sort of. I know he's dangerous. Untrustworthy. Violent. He even sold his ex-girlfriend, Marie, to a drug dealer. She was a former prostitute I knew. That is how I recognized Georgios, also known as Mr. Snake, and the reason why I declined our date yesterday."

Fear fell over Martine's face. "We need to get to the hospital right away," she said.

Anika nodded, a knot of dread tightening in her stomach. "I'll go with you!" she replied urgently.

Mishka had been attacked and she had no idea what her condition was. Anika's thoughts began to swirl again: *Why did this have to happen to her? Mishka didn't deserve to be treated like this. How can I help her?* She was reminded of her assault and the intense recovery process she endured to get through it.

That's when it hit her: Anika realized the true inspiration behind the crown painting. The artwork symbolized Mishka's strength and power. Even though she had been battered and abused, Anika believed Mishika would recover and eventually become the queen she was meant to be. This pitfall would not keep her from achieving her destiny–Anika was going to make sure of that. Since she had already agreed to go to the hospital, Anika decided she would give Mishka the canvas as a gift–a small gesture to offer comfort and connection.

Just as they were about to leave the building, Anika stopped and turned to Madam Martine, "Wait! Before we leave, I need to get something from my room first."

Without waiting for a reply, she hurried to her room and slipped into a more presentable outfit. As she turned to leave, she carefully tucked the painted canvas of Mishka's portrait under her shirt. Returning to the front, she met Martine with a steady breath.

"I'm ready, Madam Martine. And...I brought a small gift for Mishka." With that, Anika followed her out of the building and into the waiting car.

Moment of Truth

The drive to the hospital was silent except for the hum of the engine. Anika's mind raced. *If Mishka really was at the hospital, what had happened to her? And if Georgios was involved, how could they prove it?* She was anxious to get to the hospital to find out what really happened.

When they arrived, they went straight to the reception desk. Madam Martine introduced herself and explained the situation. The receptionist looked sympathetic but firm.

"I'm sorry, but I can't disclose patient information unless it's granted from the patient or you're listed as a family member," the receptionist said.

However, Madam Martine wasn't one to back down easily. "Look, this is urgent. She's an employee of mine, and we believe her life may be in danger. We need to know if she's here and if she's safe."

The receptionist hesitated, then lowered her voice. "I can tell you this much–there is a patient named Mishka who was brought in last night. She's stable for now. We've just run a couple of tests, and everything appears to be okay at the moment. She's in room 214."

Anika felt a small sense of relief. At least she was still alive.

"Can we see her?" Madam Martine asked.

The receptionist nodded. "Go ahead, but keep it brief."

Thankful for her help, Anika and Madam Martine walked down the sterile hallway to room 214. When they entered, they found Mishka lying in bed, her face swollen and bruised, her arms covered in cuts and scratches. She looked fragile, like a shadow of the bold woman Anika had seen just last night.

Anika approached the bed cautiously. "Mishka," she said softly.

Mishka's eyes fluttered open. She winced as she tried to focus on Anika and Martine. Her voice was barely audible. Suddenly, tears began to stream down her face. Weakly, she mouthed, "It was *him*...Mr. Snake. He did *this* to me."

Anika felt her chest tighten. There it was—the confirmation they had been waiting for. They could take action now, but a bigger challenge was at stake: ensuring Georgios faced justice for what he had done.

Seeing her in pain, Martine stepped forward and offered her condolences. "I'm so sorry this happened to you, sweetie. Please know that I'm here for you, and I promise to follow up on this. Oh—hold on a moment, my phone is ringing. It's the compliance officer from Luxury World. I have a meeting with him soon about what happened last night, so I'm sure he's calling to confirm. I'll be right back, Mishka," she said.

Heading out into the hallway, Madam Martine left the room to take her call. Alone with Mishka, Anika slowly took out the painting that was tucked under her shirt. Smiling gently, she handed it to her. Staring at the photo, tears streamed down Mishka's face again.

"Anika, this is so beautiful," she said. "You made this!? What a beautiful *crown*. You know, it reminds me of how valuable I am." She paused, taking a moment to catch her breath. "It makes me feel like maybe I could be something more than what I've been, you know? This painting speaks to me deeply."

Anika nodded, her heart warming at Mishka's vulnerability. "That's precisely what drew me to give you this painting. A while ago, I went through a similar situation. I want you to know that no matter what's happened or where we've been, we all deserve to feel valued—like queens of our own lives."

Quickly rubbing the tears out of her eyes, Mishka perked up a bit. "I guess I owe you one," she said, attempting to sound casual. "I'm not good at this whole...gratitude thing. But thanks."

"You don't owe me anything," Anika replied. "Just take care of yourself. That's all I want."

"I really appreciate that, Anika. Oh, and speaking of painting–I overheard someone in the hospital say there's a big art event happening this week in Nevada. Now that I know you're a painter, I think you should definitely check it out."

"Thanks, Mishka. I'll definitely look into it."

Suddenly, Madam Martine walked back into the room. Eyeing the painting, she said, "Oh my, Mishka! What a beautiful gift!"

"Thanks! It's from Anika," she replied. "Apparently she's an artist."

Immediately, Martine's expression changed. "Well, I think it's time for us to head back. Anika has some work to do." Turning to Anika, her expression became shadowed with suspicion. "There are some things I'd like to discuss with you on the way back," she said, eyeing the exit.

Anika already knew what this was about–a conversation she had been anticipating ever since Mishka received the painting. Even though it was technically her day off, she nodded her head, understandably. Inside, Anika mentally prepared for the worst.

"I'm so glad to see you recovering, sweetheart," Martine said to Mishka. "I will be in touch with the next steps, okay? Get well soon."

Anika and Madam Martine wrapped Mishka in a warm hug before turning to leave. Following Madam Martine out the door, Anika turned once more to meet Mishka's gaze. With a grateful smile, Mishka silently thanked her once more for the life-changing gift.

In the car ride back to Luxury World, Martine broke the silence.

"So, Anika...what were you and Mishka talking about?"

Anika kept her gaze ahead. "I was just telling her about the canvas I gave her. Why?"

Martine hesitated, her tone shifting. "I don't know. I get the feeling you're quite talkative with clients–and maybe even with some of my employees. But with me? You're quiet. Distant. Are you hiding something from me?"

Anika replied calmly, without looking at her. "I have nothing to hide, Madam Martine."

A heavy silence followed, thick with unspoken tension. The rest of the drive passed without another word. Anika couldn't wait to get out of Martine's car–every second felt heavier than the last. Peace was the last thing she felt.

The Final Showdown

Back at Luxury World, Anika walked to her room in deep thought. Leaving the hospital, she realized something profound. Even in a world as transactional and cutthroat as this one, kindness and compassion could still ripple outwards, creating change in unexpected ways. The thought stayed with her as she picked up her paintbrush once more, ready to pour her emotions into her art.

She was interrupted when Madam Martine suddenly knocked on Anika's room door. As soon as Anika opened it, she was met with fury.

"Anika," Martine said coldly, "I'm going to ask you one last time. What did you say to Mishka?"

Anika stood her ground, her heartbeat quickening. "I didn't say anything wrong. I just painted something for her. She's been through a lot, and I thought it might help her."

"Well, what exactly were you two discussing at the hospital when I left the room, Anika? It must've been *something,* because the receptionist just told me that Mishka called and put in her resignation!"

Surprisingly excited by the news, Anika took a deep breath and summoned her courage. "I mean, with all due respect, Madam Martine, Mishka made her own decision. If she wanted a better life for herself, I think that's something we should support, not punish."

Martine narrowed her eyes, her anger palpable. "Don't get self-righteous with me, Anika. You're here to work, not to inspire revolutions. Learn to keep your opinions and your paintings to *yourself.* I won't tolerate any more disruptions to my business! And I don't want to see anymore of your paintings in this building. **Is this clear**?"

Anika held Martine's gaze, refusing to look away. "Understood," she said evenly, though inside, she felt a mix of defiance and anger.

With that, Martine huffed and turned back toward the receptionist desk, muttering under her breath.

As she closed her bedroom door, Anika exhaled slowly, her body tense. She knew she'd made an enemy of Martine, but she didn't regret her actions. Mishka deserved a chance to rebuild her life, and if Anika's small act of kindness had helped her find the courage to leave, it was worth the risk.

As she walked back to her art, she resolved to keep going. She wasn't going to let Martine stifle her dreams any longer. Despite her resistance, Anika made herself a promise. Her purpose—to create, to inspire, and to uplift—would never waver.

Following Her Moral Compass

After her last encounter with Martine, Anika quickly realized her time working at Luxury World had come to an end. Hearing Martine tell her she could no longer do art was the final straw. Anika had finally resolved that prostitution was not for her–and this time, she would not be back. She quickly developed an exit strategy and vowed never to look back.

Within a few short days, Anika packed up all her belongings and left her bedroom key at the reception desk. Careful not to speak to anyone, she made her way to the nearest exit. With a final glance at the building, she walked away willingly in search of a new home. With every step further and further away, it felt like a weight had been lifted off her shoulders.

While walking down the Nevada strip, Anika contemplated her next steps. She never intended to leave the city to return to Montreal, but her work opportunities here had come to an end. She finally felt from the bondage that had entrapped her for what felt like years. Now, with a renewed mindset, she was ready to return home and embark on the next chapter of her life. She already looked forward to renewing lost relationships and picking up the art opportunities she had left behind.

Passing by the local businesses, Anika soon became exhausted from the day's travels. She found a nearby hotel to stay in temporarily while she mapped out her game plan. Later that evening, Anika remembered the art event Mishka had mentioned. After conducting some research, she discovered that it was being held at a quaint café that also served as an art gallery that night. Dressing in a simple but elegant outfit, Anika made her way to Painting Nite across town. When she arrived, she admired the walls adorned with vibrant works by local artists.

As she entered further, the warm glow of string lights and the hum of chatter welcomed her. She signed in and was guided to a table where other participants were setting up their easels and paints. The instructor, a lively woman named Camila, introduced herself and explained the evening's theme: "Rebirth." *How fitting!*

Anika smiled to herself at the serendipity of the event. She felt as though her life had entered its own phase of rebirth, shedding the old to embrace something more meaningful. Being here reminded Anika of her art class back in Montreal, how John had helped her enhance her gift, and how Mr. Dillon had given her the opportunity to profit from it. She reminisced about the happy memories she had made and how she had grown more talented. It would be nice to have that free time back now that she was no longer working for Luxury World.

As the session began, Anika found some supplies and got to work. She had no problem releasing her creative flow. Her brushstrokes were bold and deliberate, blending colors that represented hope, resilience, and renewal. She painted a phoenix rising from ashes, its wings outstretched and vibrant, embodying strength and transformation. It was a clear indication that she was embracing freedom from her past–the bondage that had once chained her down.

By the end of the session, the other participants admired her work, complimenting her on the depth and emotion it conveyed. Anika felt a deep sense of accomplishment–not because of the praise, but because the painting reflected her journey and aspirations. Before leaving the event, she exchanged contact information with a few attendees who were part of the local art scene. Though she had already decided to leave Nevada the following day, she felt grateful for the connections she had made. She was encouraged by the sense of belonging she had found in this creative community.

* * *

That night, back at the hotel, Anika carefully packed her new painting alongside her belongings. As she sat on the nearby stool, she thought about her future in Montreal. She was determined to build a life where her art and compassion could intertwine, helping others find their own paths to healing and self-discovery. For the first time in a long while, Anika felt at peace. She had rediscovered herself in the city of lights, and now, she was ready to shine brighter than ever.

Though she was hopeful for her future, Anika couldn't shake the image of Mishka's injuries. Moving to the edge of the bed, her thoughts spiraled, heavy and relentless. A deep ache settled in her chest—grief tangled with fury. *How could a world like this let monsters walk free? Would Martine still help Mishka get justice now that she was no longer working at Luxury World? Would Mishka recover from her injuries and embrace a new career path?* These were questions Anika wanted answers to. She decided she would get in touch with her to find out.

After making a few lengthy calls, Anika found a reliable phone number for Mishka. She called her and was happy to hear that Mishka was on the road to recovery. After her near-death encounter, Mishka decided to move back in with her parents. She wanted to return to school in the future to pursue a degree in nursing.

Thrilled by the news, Anika congratulated her and offered her full support. Though she hadn't received justice from the assault yet (Mr. Snake had left town, never to be seen or heard from again), she was learning to forgive him one day at a time. By the end of the call, Mishka and Anika vowed to stay in close touch—their bond unshaken by time or distance. Forged through shared hardship and unwavering support, their friendship reminded Anika that even in the darkest places, the seeds of hope could still take root and bloom.

Inspired by the phone call, Anika opened her sketchpad. Though it was very late, she began to draw, letting her emotions flow through the pencil in her hand. The image that emerged was raw and haunting–a shattered chain symbolizing the breaking of bonds that enslaved people, with a figure standing tall in the distance, illuminated by the light. It wasn't her usual style, but it was cathartic.

While sketching, she thought about the path she wanted to take. Mishka's story only solidified her resolve to help others. Anika knew she couldn't undo what had happened to Mishka. Still, she could use her art and compassion to support people in rebuilding their lives and finding strength after trauma. It was a future she looked forward to. Ignoring the numerous missed calls from Martine, Anika eventually fell asleep. She had resolved that she was headed in the right direction.

* * *

The next morning, Anika woke up early, packed her belongings, and checked out of the hotel. Double-checking her purse for all her belongings, she hailed a cab and directed it towards the airport. Though her flight was marked for Montreal, Anika admired the Nevada streets outside her window one last time.

Just then, a local women's shelter caught her eye. Excitedly, Anika asked the cab driver to pull over. She was inspired to go inside for just a moment. It would be her final gift to the city that had been her temporary home.

Walking into the shelter, Anika met with management and donated some of the cash she had earned from the brothel. Neglecting to tell them her story, she left a note with a love offering instead:

"To all the brave women who find themselves here, know that you are worthy of love, respect, and happiness. You are stronger than you realize, and brighter days are ahead."

Leaving the shelter, Anika was satisfied with her small act of kindness. She hoped the money would be used to treat the women there to something special.

As she boarded the plane later that day, Anika looked out the window and smiled. Nevada had been a whirlwind of experiences–some lucrative, painful, and/or enlightening. However, it was also the place where she had rediscovered her purpose and reignited her passion for art. She was thankful for the lessons she had learned while there and looked forward to her bright future ahead.

* * *

As soon as she touched base in Montreal, Anika prepared herself to reunite with her loved ones. It had been months since she had spoken to anyone back home, but she was finally ready to catch up on everything she had left behind.

First, she reached out to Rachel and updated her on all her life developments. She apologized for disappearing and was grateful that Rachel welcomed her back with a warm embrace. Once again, their friendship had proven it could withstand the tests of time.

Next, she tried calling John–the person who had opened her eyes to her talent–but his number was disconnected. Had he changed it? The line's dead silence unnerved her. For someone who had once felt like a fixed point in her chaotic world, his absence now felt too final, too absolute. John had helped her find her purpose, her path. It was as if that had been his reason for being there all along. And now–he was gone. She had always assumed she'd be able to reconnect with him when she was ready, but that was no longer the case. The thought left her with a strange, quiet ache she couldn't name. Nonetheless, she pressed forward. Then, Anika called Mr. Dillon. Though Luxury World had enabled her to profit from a hefty savings account, she specifically wanted to follow up on the job opportunity she had abruptly left hanging. After explaining the reason behind her absence, much to her surprise, Mr. Dillon was very understanding. He told Anika he was still willing to partner with her, and they planned to reconnect sometime that week.

Last but not least, Anika called her parents. It was a conversation she had been dreading, but knew was ultimately necessary for her peaceful return. They had no idea what she had endured since walking out of their house, and facing their reactions was the hardest step of all. However, the call went better than she imagined. Anika's parents were relieved to hear she was okay and eagerly discussed plans to reunite in person. Eventually, she would visit them, but only when she was emotionally ready. *There's a time for everything,* she reminded herself. She vowed to take one day at a time for the sake of her healing.

* * *

Over the next few days, Anika used her savings to furnish her new apartment and set up a small art studio. She wasted no time working on a collection inspired by resilience and transformation. In her free time, she volunteered at local shelters, offering art therapy sessions to women who had endured abuse and exploitation. Though the journey from Montreal to Nevada and back to Montreal had been memorable, she was grateful to be back home, where she belonged.

Living with Purpose

After her phone call with Mr. Dillon, Anika made plans to reconnect with him at the Rise Hotel art gallery later that week. Appreciative of his unwavering support, she decided to move forward–she wanted to display her artwork publicly. It was a significant step for her career that would catapult her success and showcase her talent.

Over the next few weeks, Anika began attending events at different galleries, gradually becoming more involved in the art community. At the hotel where she worked, some of Anika's responsibilities included light administrative tasks, such as answering phones, responding to emails, and updating the database–especially leading up to events. On occasion, she and a few other staff members also helped install and take down exhibitions, giving her a hands-on look at what it takes to bring a show to life. The art gallery was a significant partnership within the hotel and Anika was grateful for all the connections she made through the businesses.

Months later, Anika's art began to draw increasing attention. It didn't take long before she was invited to exhibit at a local gallery's special event, a milestone that marked how far she had come. Her paintings–raw, honest, and filled with stories of struggle and resilience–resonated deeply with viewers. People not only saw the paint, but the power within her work. Empowered by the support, Anika felt good about herself. She was finally living the life she was meant to live: one rooted in healing, self-expression, and subtle empowerment.

* * *

At home, Anika continued painting, her brush gliding across the canvas with a grace that matched the tranquility in her heart. Each stroke brought the serene image of a lush forest to life, with golden sunlight breaking through the leafy canopy. It was a reflection of her newfound inner peace–a sanctuary she had created within herself despite her rocky past.

One day in particular, she paused for a moment, looking at the nearly finished painting. A soft smile spread across her face. It wasn't just a depiction of nature; it was her story, her journey toward self-acceptance and love. For years, she had sought validation in the wrong places, trying to mold herself to fit the expectations of others. But now, she understood the profound truth of the words she had once heard in church: *"Love your neighbor as yourself."*

Somehow, she had missed the first part of that wisdom: the necessity of loving herself *first*. Without self-love, how could she genuinely love or help others? This revelation had been her turning point. Saying "no" to what didn't align with her true self had been difficult, but it was liberating. It allowed her to say yes to what truly mattered–healing, growth, and authenticity.

Her thoughts drifted to the people she had encountered on her journey. They included Mishka, some of the clients she connected with from the brothel, and John, the kind, art mentor from the coffee shop she had lost touch with. Each interaction had taught her something valuable about herself and the world. They reminded Anika that love wasn't just about grand gestures or romance. It was about kindness, understanding, and the courage to stand by one's values.

* * *

That night, as the clock struck 2 am, Anika added the final touches to her painting. A single ray of light pierced through the trees, illuminating a small path that led deeper into the forest. It symbolized hope and the promise of new beginnings. She leaned back and admired her work. It wasn't perfect, but it didn't need to be. It was honest, just like her.

As she cleaned up and finally got into bed, she felt an overwhelming sense of gratitude. Gratitude for the lessons learned, the strength to walk away from what no longer served her, and the courage to embrace who she truly was. For the first time in years, Anika felt whole. She didn't know what the future held, but she was no longer afraid. She had finally found her peace, and with it, a love that would guide her through whatever came next.

CHAPTER 7
Walking in Freedom

The next morning, Anika arrived at the Rise Hotel with a mix of excitement and nervousness. She had been excelling in her position and found her workload easy to navigate. Noticing her potential for more, Mr. Dillon approached her with another job opportunity. As one of the board members at the local community center, he learned there was a vacancy for a youth art teacher. After sharing this with Anika, he was thrilled that she had accepted the part-time position on the spot. The thought of teaching young people how to paint filled her with a sense of purpose. It was a far cry from her previous life, and she was determined to make the most of this opportunity.

Mr. Dillon greeted her warmly at the entrance. "Anika, it's so good to see you!" he said, giving him a genuine hug. "You look radiant. How have you been?"

"I've been...rediscovering myself," Anika replied with a smile. "And I think this job is exactly what I need right now."

Mr. Dillon nodded his head in agreement. He was thankful to have Anika's talented hands contributing to the program's success and looked forward to supporting her along the way. Leaving the hotel, they caught a cab and rode together to the community center. Along the way, Mr. Dillon did his best to share as many details about the position with her as possible.

As part of her training, Mr. Dillon gave Anika a tour of the facility. The first stop was a newly renovated room used for art classes. It was bright and inviting, with large windows letting in natural light. Easels were set up in rows, and shelves filled with paints, brushes, and blank canvases lined the walls. A sense of calm and creativity enveloped the space.

"What do you think?" Mr. Dillon asked, his eyes sparkling with anticipation.

"It's perfect," Anika said, her voice filled with emotion. "I can already see this becoming a place of healing and expression for so many."

Mr. Dillon smiled. "I knew you'd feel that way. You have such a gift, Anika. Not just with painting but with connecting to people. That's why I thought this would be perfect for you."

Anika walked around the room, touching the easels and feeling the smooth surface of the canvases. Her mind raced with ideas for lessons and workshops. She imagined young people coming here not only to learn the art of painting but also to find their voice, just as she had found hers.

As Anika walked along, she paused to watch a young man brush bold strokes of turquoise across the wall. Feeling the urge to introduce herself, she said, "Hello—I'm Anika!"

Tilting his head, the young man smiled and set his brush down. "Very nice to meet you. I'm Diego."

Anika tucked a strand of hair behind her ear. "Thank you for painting this room. You're doing a great job."

Diego picked up his brush again and let out a soft chuckle. "Oh, you're very welcome. Mr. Dillon asked me to make this place look beautiful–it's my pleasure."

As they continued the tour, Anika turned to see Mr. Dillon leaning in slightly. His voice low, but warm, he said, "Diego's wonderful–he's smart, talented, and quite well-known back in Cuba. It's a shame he's only here temporarily. He works with his family there and they run a business together." Mr. Dillon's eyes crinkled with affection as he spoke, clearly fond of Diego.

Whispering back, Anika responded, "Something is fascinating about him. I'll definitely ask more about his artwork soon."

"Good for you, Anika! Your artwork here is incredible, so connecting with other artists will only take you further," Mr. Dillon said with a grin.

"Thank you for believing in me," she said, turning to Mr. Dillon. "This means more to me than you can imagine."

"Of course," Mr. Dillon replied. "You're going to do amazing things here. And remember, I'm always here if you need anything."

* * *

Anika spent the rest of the day at the community center preparing for her first workshop. She sketched out lesson plans, gathered materials, and brainstormed themes that could inspire creativity and self-discovery in her students. For the first time in a long time, she felt a sense of hope. It marked the beginning of a new chapter–a chapter where she could give back, inspire others, and live authentically. It was a future she could not help but look forward to.

That evening, Anika prepared for closing time. As she was about to leave the workshop area, Anika whispered to herself, *"This is where I'm meant to be."*

Waving goodbye to Mr. Dillon, Anika found herself lingering in the hallway near the art room. She could still hear the faint sound of Diego's brush strokes drifting against the nearby wall. He had remained at the community center all this time, working long after hours.

Anika admired his dedication. Something was intriguing about him—his confident yet humble demeanor, his passion for art, and, of course, his radiant smile that had made her feel flustered. Anika took a deep breath and decided to reenter the room. She told herself it was to observe the progress of the renovations, but deep down, she was curious about Diego.

"Hey! You're still here!?" Diego said with a grin as he noticed her walk in. He was standing on a ladder, putting the finishing touches on a vibrant mural.

"Yes," she replied, her voice softer than she intended. "I just wanted to see how everything was coming along. It's looking great."

"Thank you. It's a nice space. Perfect for what you're going to do here," Diego said, climbing down the ladder. "Teaching kids to paint is a beautiful way to make a difference."

Anika nodded. "It feels like the right thing to do. Art helped me through some tough times, and I think it can do the same for them."

Diego wiped his hands on a rag and gave her an encouraging look. "That's the power of art. It can heal, inspire, and connect people in ways nothing else can."

Anika smiled and nodded in agreement. They stood in silence for a moment, both taking in the room and its possibilities.

"Mr. Dillon told me that you're a well-known artist in Cuba," Anika said, breaking the silence. "That must've been an incredible experience."

"It was," Diego said, his voice tinged with nostalgia. "But life has a way of pushing you in different directions. I came here to start fresh. It hasn't been easy, but I believe there's something here for me. Maybe this upcoming auction will open some doors."

Earlier that day, Mr. Dillon had told Anika that the community center was busy preparing for their annual auction later that week. It was an opportunity to showcase the artwork the members had been busy working on and establish potential business sponsorships. The auction was a significant event for the facility, which was why Mr. Dillon had urgently asked Anika for her support with the youth classes. He needed all hands on deck to ensure the auction went seamlessly well.

"I'm sure it will," Anika said knowingly with a smile. "From what I can tell, your work is amazing."

Diego chuckled. "Thanks. Maybe you'll get to see some of my other pieces someday."

"I'd like that," she said, surprising herself with her honesty.

Diego's smile widened. "Well, I should get back to work. But it was nice talking to you, Anika. I have a feeling you're going to do great things here."

"Thank you, Diego. And good luck with the auction," she said before heading out of the room.

As Anika left the center, she couldn't help but feel a spark of excitement. Meeting Diego and hearing his story inspired her even more. She felt like her new life was unfolding in unexpected and beautiful ways, and she was ready to embrace whatever came next.

Stepping outside, Anika spotted Mr. Dillon leaning against the side of the building, a cigarette between his fingers.

"Hey, Anika. Hope you get some good rest this week," he said. "Friday night will be a big day for all of us. Families and friends of the artists, as well as potential sponsors, will be visiting here. I'm inviting mine, and Diego's bringing his girlfriend too. The more people, the better, right? We need all the exposure we can get to ensure this community center maintains its integrity."

"Absolutely! I'm looking forward to the event. Thanks again for the opportunity!" she replied with a slightly disappointed smile. "*So, Diego has a girlfriend,*" she thought as she prepared to head home. The fact lingered in her mind, heavier than she expected.

What's Meant to Be

Much to Anika's surprise, Friday came quicker than expected. As the clock ticked closer to the evening event, Anika couldn't help but feel a mix of emotions–curiosity, confusion, and a hint of disappointment. She thought about what Mr. Dillon had said about Diego being in a relationship. Anika did her best to avoid Diego all week, but seeing him tonight was inevitable.

"*Maybe I'm just overthinking,*" she muttered to herself as she freshened up in the staff washroom before the event. She decided she needed some reassurance.

Anika pulled her phone from her jeans pocket and quickly dialed Rachel.

"Hey, girl!" Rachel answered, her voice warm and upbeat. "What's new!?"

After Anika filled her in on meeting Diego–and the surprising detail about him having a girlfriend–Rachel paused.

Then she said, "Look, just say 'Hi' to him, you know? As a co-worker. Whether he's single or not, don't overthink it. Just be yourself. What's meant to happen will happen, Anika."

Anika agreed and hung up the phone. Thankful for her good friend Rachel, Anika was refocused and ready for the event.

* * *

Finally, the community center staff took a step back to admire the main room. They had been preparing all day and were now ready to open the doors for the auction. Paintings were displayed on easels, and within a few minutes, the air was alive with chatter and excitement. Anika entered the room and scanned the crowd, spotting Diego near the stage. He looked confident and calm as he spoke with some of the other artists.

"Anika, over here!" Mr. Dillon waved from the other side of the room, holding a slice of pizza.

Redirecting her attention to Mr. Dillon, Anika made her way over and grabbed a slice for herself. She tried to focus on the art and the event, but her mind kept drifting back to Diego.

As the presentations began, Diego was called up to showcase his art. He walked onto the stage with a quiet confidence that drew everyone's attention. He spoke about his inspiration, his love for his homeland, Cuba, and the stories behind his pieces. His passion was evident, and the audience was captivated.

Anika watched him closely, feeling both admiration and a strange pang of longing. She shook her head, trying to focus on his words instead of her swirling thoughts.

After the presentations, the artists mingled with the guests. That's when Anika found herself standing near one of Diego's paintings–a stunning depiction of a vibrant Cuban street scene.

"You like it?" a familiar voice said from behind her.

She turned to see Diego, smiling as usual.

"It's beautiful," she said. "The colors, the details–it feels alive."

"Thank you," he said, looking genuinely pleased. "It's one of my favorites, too."

They stood in silence for a moment, taking in the painting. Then Diego spoke again.

"I'm really happy you agreed to work here with the kids, Anika."

"Thank you," Anika said, feeling a blush rise to her cheeks.

Before she could say more, a woman approached them and placed a hand on Diego's arm.

"Hey, *babe*," the woman said, smiling warmly.

"Oh, hey, Claudia," Diego said, turning to her. "This is Anika, the new art instructor here. Anika, this is Claudia, my girlfriend."

Anika felt her heart sink, but managed a polite smile. "Nice to meet you, Claudia."

"You too," Claudia said, her tone friendly.

As the two of them walked away, Anika took a deep breath and remembered what Rachel had recently told her over the phone. She had to stay focused.

A Quiet Promise

That night, Anika resolved to concentrate on her work and journey. The auction had been a resounding success, and she had heard that the community center had earned more money than in any of their past events. Before leaving, Mr. Dillon attributed part of the victory to Anika. He personally congratulated her on her contributions and reassured her that she had his unwavering support. His encouragement was exactly what she needed to hear. Whatever the future held, she knew it would unfold in its own time. For now, she had a purpose to fulfill, and that was enough.

As Anika sat on her bed, she stared at the rainbow canvas Diego had painted. She had purchased it that night and admired it resting on her night table. Internally, she felt a mix of emotions. The vibrant colors of the painting seemed to reflect a sense of hope, joy, and new beginnings—emotions she hadn't fully embraced in a long time. Diego's kind words about her joining the team at the community center warmed her heart, but she reminded herself to keep her personal feelings about him in check.

"He was being nice, that's all," she said aloud, trying to temper her thoughts.

Anika got up and placed the painting on her dresser, allowing it to stand where she could admire it more easily. It was a reminder of her new chapter—a symbol of how far she'd come and the possibilities ahead.

Sitting at her small desk, she grabbed her notebook and began to jot down ideas for her future art classes. Her mind buzzed with lesson plans and projects she could do with the kids. She wanted to create a space where they could express themselves freely, just as painting had become her refuge during her darkest times.

The sound of her phone vibrating on the table snapped her out of her thoughts. She picked it up and saw a message from Mr. Dillon:

"Anika, once again, you did great tonight. Diego said it was nice chatting with you. You left quite an impression on him. Rest well. See you tomorrow!"

Anika smiled, her heart fluttering just a little.

Praying aloud, she said, *"If Diego is part of your plan for me, I will let it happen naturally."*

She closed her notebook and leaned back, staring at the painting once more. The rainbow seemed to shine with a quiet promise–a reminder that storms pass and the aftermath is often beautiful. With that thought, Anika turned off her bedside lamp and lay down on her bed. Her heart was lit with hope, and her spirit was ready for whatever the next day would bring.

Where Art Meets Heart

A month into her new role as an art teacher, Anika found herself enjoying every moment. Working with the children revealed qualities she didn't know she had–patience, adaptability, and a natural ability to inspire creativity. Each class presented its own set of challenges, but witnessing the joy on the children's faces made it all worthwhile.

Still, there were moments when a quiet ache surfaced–especially during story time or when a child reached out for a comforting hand. Just a few months earlier, she'd had an abortion. It had been the hardest decision of her life, made after sleepless nights, wavering between fear and responsibility. In the clinic, she had felt alone, hollow, and uncertain. The sterile walls there were unable to contain the storm inside her. Yet, in the aftermath–through the grief, the guilt, and the quiet resolve–she never questioned the necessity of her choice. She carried it with her now, not as a shadow, but as a scar. Healed over, yet still tender.

Being with the children somehow helped her breathe a little easier, even as it stirred a complex mix of sorrow and peace.

"This is better than homework!" a cheerful boy exclaimed during one session.

Anika chuckled. "I'll take that as a compliment."

* * *

One evening, as she was packing up her supplies at the community center, Diego appeared at the door. Following the auction's success, Mr. Dillon offered her a full-time position as the lead art teacher. Realizing that teaching had become her calling, she accepted his offer gratefully.

"You're a great teacher," he said with a warm smile.

"Oh, *thank you*," she replied, flattered and a little surprised to see him.

"Are you free tonight?" Diego asked, his voice gentle. "There's a cozy coffee shop just across the street. Maybe you've been there. It's called the Blooming Café. I'd really like it if you joined me."

Anika paused, her eyes searching his, "Don't you have a *girlfriend*, Diego?"

He shook his head softly. "We broke up over a month ago. Since then, I've been in therapy, focusing on growth and developing my art. You know, healing."

Anika studied him for a moment, then gave a slight nod, a flicker of a smile forming. The news was music to her ears, but she chose her following words carefully, "I can certainly relate to that! Good for you for taking time to heal." Softly reaching over to touch his hand, she added, "Yes–I'd love to hang out."

* * *

At the café, they found a quiet corner to sit and talk. Diego was easy to converse with, and Anika quickly realized how much they had in common. Their shared love for painting sparked lively discussions about famous artists.

"Whenever I think about Pablo Picasso," Anika said, "his work always feels like a glimpse into his personal thoughts. Similarly, I've been storing my paintings almost like a personal journal. It's been therapeutic."

Diego nodded. "I can see that. For me, Henri Matisse resonates the most. He once said, 'I am unable to make any distinction between the feeling I get from life and the way I translate that feeling into painting.' And that's exactly how I feel when I create something with my hands."

Anika smiled, appreciating the depth of his passion. "It's amazing how painting is not just art but an extension of who we are."

Diego leaned back and grinned. He couldn't agree more. "You know, we're both pretty passionate about this. Why not work together on building something? Maybe an *art business*?"

Anika laughed, unsure if he was serious or simply brainstorming aloud. "That's a bold idea, Diego. But who knows!? Maybe one day."

As a brief silence settled between them, Diego spoke up gently. "You know, there's an exhibition tomorrow night at Soleil Park. It's supposed to be amazing. Would you like to go with me?"

Without hesitation, Anika exclaimed, "I'd love to! It'll also be a great chance for us to network with other artists."

"Absolutely," Diego agreed with a smile.

As their conversation continued, Anika felt a connection forming between them. Diego was not just talented but kind, thoughtful, and full of vision. She didn't know where this would lead, but for the first time in a long while, she felt she was exactly where she needed to be–exploring new possibilities with art and her heart.

True Colors, True Connection

The next day, Anika woke up with a sense of excitement. The conversation with Diego replayed in her mind, and the thought of their upcoming date brought a smile to her face. She hadn't felt this lighthearted in a long time, and it was refreshing. Diego's thoughtfulness and genuine manner–and the sweet nervousness he showed when asking her out–only made him even more endearing.

As she prepared for the day, she marveled at how far she'd come emotionally and spiritually. Once someone who made impulsive decisions, including working as a sex worker, she was now embracing life as an artist and living her dreams. Her transformation felt nothing short of extraordinary.

As Anika continued to reflect on her conversation with Diego, she realized how deeply her perspective on relationships had evolved. What once felt fraught and uncertain now held the promise of authenticity and connection. She was no longer willing to settle for anything less than mutual respect and understanding. She had learned to love herself more, and that made her selective about who she allowed into her life.

* * *

On their date, Anika met Diego at the exhibit he had mentioned the day before. Drifting from piece to piece, their eyes lit up as they traced the interplay of shades and textures in the artworks. Diego leaned in, voice soft and sincere, pointing out how the teal in one painting seemed to shift toward jade under the gallery lights.

Anika chuckled, retelling a moment from her day with the kids. Apparently, one student had declared a "masterpiece" after spilling paint all over their canvas! Amused by the memory, the couple burst into laughter, the sound echoing in the high-ceilinged space.

Their conversation was deceptively simple: casual color notes and offhand jokes. Yet, every word carried weight. Diego's openness and the warmth behind his laughter, revealed a sincerity that resonated with her. In comparison to past relationships–so often one-sided or surface-level–this felt refreshingly real. As the date went on, Anika grew increasingly excited about the possibility of love. The process of forming a genuine connection with someone who valued her for who she truly was made her feel overcome with joy.

* * *

After the exhibit ended, Diego offered Anika a ride home. As they drove through the quiet streets, conversation flowed easily between them, each moment drawing them closer. Anika felt a gentle nudge in her heart. She turned to Diego, her eyes reflecting both vulnerability and resolve, and spoke with quiet conviction. "I want to use art to heal people," she said. "Not just to create beauty, but to help others find something in themselves–peace, maybe, or hope.

Diego listened closely, his gaze steady and thoughtful, the weight of her words settling between them. "That's an incredible vision, Anika," he said warmly. "You're absolutely right–there's so much untapped potential in people. Sometimes, all it takes is someone to believe in them and help them find their way. If anyone can do that, it's you."

Anika smiled, grateful for his encouragement. "Thank you, Diego. I've been through so much. I know what it feels like to feel stuck, like there's no way out. I want to give women hope, a safe place to heal, and a chance to start over through art education."

Diego nodded. "You've already started doing that with the kids you're teaching. Expanding it to women would be a natural next step. If you decide to open an art school, let me know–I'll do whatever I can to support you." He paused, then continued. "Which leads me to something I've been wanting to talk to you about. I am deeply saddened to say that I will be leaving soon to go back to Cuba."

Anika was overcome with emotion. Her previous conversation with Mr. Dillon about Diego returning to Cuba one day came flooding back into her memory. Somehow, in between all the time they had spent together, she had forgotten this key detail. Now, hearing Diego's kind and supportive words made her heart ache. Diego had become a source of refreshment. His presence had revived her–yet, the knowledge of his departure hung over her like a shadow she couldn't outrun.

"Wow, I guess I forgot all about that. Thank you for telling me, Diego," she said softly, her voice tinged with emotion. "Mr. Dillon told me you'd go back home at some point. I just…I wish you didn't have to go so soon."

Diego sighed, his tone softening. "I wish I could stay too. You've made these last few weeks unforgettable, Anika. But my family and work are in Cuba. It's not just about me–I have responsibilities there I have to attend to."

Unable to look at him, Anika stared out the window. Her thoughts swirled. She admired Diego's maturity but couldn't help feeling disappointed. "I understand. It's just, well, I guess…" Anika struggled to find the words. "I hoped we'd have more time to figure things out together."

Diego reached for her hand, his touch warm and reassuring. "We still can," he said gently. "If you're open to it, I'd like to continue what we've started. I know we'll be far apart, but my hope is that the distance won't become a wall between us."

Anika nodded, holding back tears. She did her best to push aside the ache in her chest. "You're right," she said softly. "Let's just make the most of the time we have. I look forward to whatever comes next."

As the car slowed to a stop in front of her apartment, Diego turned to her with a gentle smile, his eyes filled with quiet sincerity. "Anika, no matter where I am, promise me you'll keep chasing your dreams. You're meant to do incredible things—I believe in you."

"Thank you, Diego. That means everything to me," she said, her voice filled with emotion.

As she stepped out of the car and watched him drive away, Anika resolved to focus on her vision. That night, as she turned off her phone and prepared to sleep, Anika whispered a quiet prayer of gratitude. She thanked God for the opportunities and people who had entered her life. Tomorrow was another chance to explore something new, and she was ready to embrace what was ahead. She didn't know what the future held for her and Diego, but she knew one thing for sure—her purpose was bigger than her circumstances.

Purpose Over Circumstance

It had been several months since Diego left for Cuba, but not a day went by that he didn't think of Anika. Realizing his heart belonged with her, he returned—not just to visit, but to stay close to the woman he loved. Thrilled by his long-term presence, Anika found herself falling deeper in love with him.

One evening, as the sun painted the sky in shades of gold and rose, they wandered hand in hand through a quiet park. With the soft hush of twilight around them, Diego turned to Anika. Dropping to one knee, he asked her to spend forever with him.

She responded with an astounding, "YES!"

A few days later, with the ring still catching light on her finger, they drove together through familiar streets that hadn't felt like home in years. The car hummed softly beneath them, but the energy inside was charged—a blend of excitement for what they were building together, and a quiet tension about what lay ahead. Anika hadn't spoken to her parents in years, and now she was returning not just as a daughter, but as a fiancée. Her mind raced with questions: *Would they welcome her? Would they forgive her distance? Could they accept the woman she had become?* Only time would tell.

As the car weaved through the streets toward Anika's childhood home, the energy inside the vehicle was a mix of excitement and nervous anticipation. Anika's heart raced as she stared at the engagement ring, the sparkling reminder of the bold step she was about to take. Diego sat beside her, calm yet supportive, his reassuring hand resting on hers.

When they were a few minutes out, Anika decided to video-call her childhood friend, Rachel. The screen flickered for a moment before Rachel's face appeared, framed by a messy bun. The familiar chaos of her apartment displayed behind her.

"Hey, stranger," Rachel grinned. "It's been *forever*! What's the big news you were being all cryptic about?"

Anika hesitated for just a breath, then held up her hand to the camera, the ring catching the light.

Rachel leaned in, squinting, then froze. "Is that…what I *think* it is?"

Anika smiled, half-hopeful, half-bracing. "Yup! I'm engaged."

Rachel's eyes widened, and for a second, her face was unreadable, "To *who?*"

Anika laughed nervously. "His name is Diego. Remember, I had mentioned him a while back? I know, I know–I never formally introduced you to him. Things moved quickly, and I wanted to be sure before I–"

"Wait, wait." Rachel held up her hand and sat back. "You're telling me...you've been dating Diego *seriously* enough to marry him, and you haven't told me more about him until *now*?" Rachel was clearly confused.

"I didn't want to rush you into judging someone you hadn't met yet," Anika said, more gently. "I was scared of what you'd say. I was scared you'd talk me out of it before I had the chance to trust him for myself. A lot has changed since we first started working together."

Rachel was quiet for a minute. Then, with a half-sigh, half-laugh, she muttered, "I can respect that." She paused before adding, "Wow–you really did it. You fell off the radar and came back with a fiancé. You really *are* talented, girl!"

Anika laughed nervously. "Does that mean you're still mad at me?"

Rachel shook her head, the corners of her mouth twitching. "No. Just shocked and a little hurt. Except for the last few months, we've been through every chapter of life together. I thought I'd be there for this milestone too."

Anika's eyes softened. "And you still can be! Listen, I know I've been working a lot and some things have changed, but you will *always* be a part of my life. I want you to meet Diego tomorrow. I won't move forward without your blessing!"

Rachel looked at her best friend through the screen for a long moment, then gave a small, crooked smile. "Okay, but he better be **amazing**. And if he's not. I'm coming to the wedding anyway to object dramatically."

Anika laughed, the tension lifting. "*Deal.*"

Directing her voice towards Diego (who was visibly noticeable in the driver's seat), Rachel called out, "Pleasure to meet you!" With a playful smile, her eyes narrowed slightly as she studied him through the screen.

"Pleasure is mine, Ms. Rachel! I look forward to meeting you in person soon." Diego responded charmingly, careful not to take his attention away from the road.

Rachel nodded with approval before turning her attention back to Anika. Eyebrows raised, she said, "Okay, Anika, *spill*. When exactly did all this happen? I can't believe you've been keeping secrets from me!?"

Anika let out a nervous laugh, her cheeks flushed. "I promise I will fill you in on all the details. For now, I'll say that it all happened *fast*!. One minute, we were just friends. Best friends, really. And then–somehow–it all just clicked. It feels like it was meant to be."

Rachel's expression softened as she listened. The tension between surprise and excitement slowly gave way to genuine happiness.

Diego smiled at her, his eyes warm and kind. Reaching over, he softly rubbed her hand. "It's true. Anika's been a blessing in my life. I couldn't wait any longer to make her my wife."

Admiring their love story, Rachel grinned at the screen. "That is so beautiful! You two are perfect together. I'm so happy for you guys–truly."

After chatting a little longer, they exchanged goodbyes. Promising to meet up the next day, they ended the call. The timing was perfect as they had just pulled into Anika's parents' driveway.

Homecoming

Diego turned off the car and removed the keys from the ignition. The humming sound of the engine settling filled the quiet between them. As they stared at Anika's childhood home, a sudden wave of nerves hit Anika stronger than she'd expected. She found herself holding her breath in nervousness. The sight of the old porch, the garden her mother used to fuss over, the wind chimes softly clinking in the breeze–it all came rushing back. She hadn't been home in over a year, and now she was returning with life-changing news. Anika prayed she would be welcomed back with open arms.

As her fingers fidgeted in her lap, Diego, ever attentive, noticed the tension in her jawline. He watched her eyes linger on the front door–it was clear she was nervous. Gently, he leaned in and whispered, "Hey, you've got this. I'm right here with you." His voice was steady and warm–like a hand gently placed on her back, quietly urging her forward.

Anika took a deep breath and gripped Diego's hand one last time for strength. She slipped her phone into her bag and got out of the car. With Diego present beside her, Anika breathed in the late afternoon air. It was warm–tinged with the scent of jasmine from her mother's garden. The sight of her peaceful neighborhood brought back some of her best childhood memories. Yet, each step up the driveway felt heavier than the last and strangely grounding.

Before they could reach the front door, it swung open. Anika's father stood in the entryway, his eyes instantly lit up with joy.

"Anika!" he exclaimed, arms already open. "Anika! My girl, you're back!" He pulled her into a tight hug, his embrace warm and forgiving.

"Hi, Dad," Anika said, her voice trembling with emotion.

Just then, her mother appeared in the doorway, her expression a mix of surprise and cautious hope. "Anika…" she said softly.

"Mom," Anika began, holding back tears, "I'm sorry for everything. I've missed you both so much."

Her mother paused for only a moment, eyes filling with emotion, before she opened her arms wide. "Come here, sweetheart."

Anika didn't hesitate. She rushed into her mother's embrace, sinking into the familiar warmth and comfort she'd missed so deeply. Tears fell from her face uncontrollably. It felt like she was coming home in every sense of the word.

After a long, quiet moment, Anika's mother pulled back just enough to look at her face. Her eyes were shining. "Look at you," she said softly, brushing a strand of hair behind Anika's ear. "You're glowing." Noticing Diego standing nearby, she said, "And who's this?"

"Mom, Dad, this is Diego," Anika said, her voice steady. "My fiancé."

Her parents exchanged surprised looks, then smiled warmly. Her father stepped forward to shake Diego's hand. "Fiancé, huh?" They were clearly in shock. "Well, welcome to the family, Diego."

"Thank you, sir," Diego said politely.

Her mother looked at Anika with tears in her eyes. "This is wonderful news, Anika. I'm so proud of you."

* * *

The reunion was filled with laughter, introductions, and conversations that felt like a fresh start for Anika and her family. For the first time in a long time, Anika felt truly at peace, surrounded by love and hope for the future. The room buzzed with excitement as the news of Anika and Diego's engagement settled in. A lot had changed since she had been gone. It appeared that Anika's absence had rekindled a flame between her parents. They appeared happier and more in tune than ever. Anika felt a wave of relief wash over her—her parents' warmth and acceptance were more than she had dared to hope for.

Then, her mother clasped her hands together. "Oh, I can't believe this day has finally come! We're going to have so much to plan—wedding details, guest lists, dresses..." she trailed off, already mentally diving into preparations.

Diego chuckled softly. "We're definitely open to ideas, ma'am. I want Anika to have the wedding of her dreams."

Anika smiled at him, squeezing his hand. "Thank you, Diego. And mom, you know I'll need your help—just not *tonight*," she teased.

Anika's dad especially beamed with excitement. With a satisfied smile on his face, he said, "Well, looks like our prayers were answered! Once again, Diego, welcome to the family. If there's one thing I can say, it's that you're marrying an incredible woman."

Diego nodded. "Thank you, Dwayne. I know. I'm fortunate."

* * *

As the evening continued, a light atmosphere of laughter and conversation filled the house. Diego shared stories of his upbringing in Cuba and how art had always been his passion. Anika's parents, in turn, spoke about Anika's childhood, bringing up funny and touching memories that made Anika's cheeks flush with embarrassment.

When a few hours had passed, Anika's mother excused herself to the kitchen, where she began preparing tea and some light snacks. She returned with a tray and set it on the coffee table. Thanking her for her gracious hospitality, Diego and Anika accepted the delicious treats offered to them. As they took a moment to glance around the room, a wave of joy washed over them. Anika's family was warm, happy, and wholly supportive. The gathering, united in celebration, felt like a sign that everything was falling into place. The comforting warmth of the family home was contagious, and it was clear her parents had healed the fractures in their own relationship. For the first time in years, Anika felt truly—and deeply—at home.

* * *

At the height of Anika's homecoming, Diego leaned close and softly reassured her, "You deserve all the happiness in the world."

She met his gaze, smiling back as her heart swelled with warmth.

Noticing the joyful couple, Anika's father stood and fixed his eyes on her. "Anika, your mother and I would like to speak with you privately, please."

Curious, Anika followed them from the living room to the kitchen, while Diego waited patiently on the couch.

Sitting at the kitchen table, her father began. "Your mother and I want to apologize, Anika," his voice was low but steady. "Before you left, we did what we thought was right at the time. We truly believed we were guiding you the best way we knew how." He paused, eyes searching hers. "But somewhere along the way, in our effort to uphold the rules of this house—and the faith we built our lives around—we lost sight of something far more important: your heart. Since you've been gone, we've had a lot of time to think. For all the times you felt alone under this roof, we truly apologize."

Her mother reached over, gently placing her hand over Anika's. "We've missed you more than you know. And your siblings have, too."

Anika's father offered a small, hopeful smile. "The kids are upstairs sleeping now, but I really wish they could've seen you. Hopefully, this won't be your last visit."

Suddenly, the sound of footsteps quietly echoed, and giggles could be heard coming from the adjoining staircase to the kitchen. Michael and Riley had already made their way down, unable to resist the familiar voice they'd heard. Much to their father's surprise, they hadn't been asleep after all.

Before Anika and Diego arrived, Michael had been playing video games on his tablet, while Riley scrolled through her social media feed. Though they were supposed to be asleep, they both were too curious—and too awake—to miss what was happening downstairs.

Peeking around the corner, Michael's eyes widened in surprise. Meanwhile, his sister, Riley, ran down from behind him and threw herself into Anika's arms, sobbing.

"WHERE HAVE YOU BEEN!?" she cried, clinging tightly. "We've been praying nonstop for you to come back!"

Anika held her close, her own throat tightening with emotion.

Moments later, Michael rushed over, wiping at his eyes as he joined the embrace. "I'm glad you're here, Anika," he said quietly. "When you left, there was a huge hole in this house. It hasn't felt the same since."

Tears welled in Anika's eyes as she looked at the two of them—no longer the little kids she remembered. In her absence, they had grown into people with hearts wide open. For a moment, a flicker of doubt passed through her—*had she left too soon? Had she abandoned her siblings?* These thoughts ran through her mind until she looked over and glanced at Diego.

And that's when it hit her. Everything she had gone through had shaped her into who she was today. That long, painful, winding road led her to the love of her life and restored relationships. Anika was stronger now than she had even been in the past. Leaving home was the catalyst that set it all in motion. Her redemption story had brought her back home with a wholeness she never could've imagined. Despite her suffering, Anika had bloomed into a beautiful woman inside and outside.

Noticing another opportunity to celebrate, Anika's mother ushered her family back into the living room. Hurrying back into the kitchen, she later returned carrying a tray of elegant champagne glasses. Each one was filled with sparkling juice. Moments later, her father followed suit with a bottle of non-alcoholic champagne (honoring the family's long-held tradition).

After Diego was introduced to Anika's siblings and everyone was settled into their seats, her mother raised her glass, a gentle smile on her face. "Let us toast–not just to the engagement, but to the journey that brought us here. Anika, you look radiant. You've grown into such a strong, responsible woman. And Diego," she turned to him warmly, "thank you for loving her so well, and for treating her the way she deserves."

Adding to the toast, Anika's father lifted his glass, "We stand together as a family and welcome you, Diego. As long as you take care of our Anika, you are not just accepted–you are embraced. You're now part of this family."

Michael grinned and nudged Diego playfully. Their brotherly bond was already forming.

"This is awesome! Welcome to the family, Diego. I can't believe I have a new older brother!"

Diego chuckled, clearly touched, and gave a nod of humility. "It's an honor–truly. Thank you all for welcoming me. I promise to cherish Anika, to stand by her, and to walk with her through every step of life."

Clinking their drinks gently, the family sipped their celebratory drinks with excitement. For the first time in years, the room felt full of love, belonging, and sacred healing.

As the night drew to a close, Anika felt an overwhelming sense of gratitude. She had dreamed of a moment like this, but never imagined it would feel so real, so soon. Yet, this was her reality: restored family, present life, and a bright future. Though she and her family had a lot of catching up to do, Anika was excited about the healing process.

* * *

On the car ride back, Anika reflected on her life. She had walked through darkness, doubt, and distance, but every step had led her to this moment–to a place of purpose, love, and belonging. The pain she once carried had shaped her, but it no longer defined her. Surrounded by the love of her family, the support of her friends, and the quiet strength of a man who believed in her, she finally understood that healing wasn't just about moving on–it was about rebuilding something new from the pieces left behind.

With her heart full and her vision clear, Anika knew this was only the beginning. Ahead of her lay more than a wedding, the potential to further her art education, or the fulfillment of her dreams for a women's center; instead, it was a life rooted in compassion and resilience. Her life lessons had taught her that pressure was essential in producing diamonds. Looking forward, Anika was no longer scared of her future. Now more than ever, she was fully prepared to *bloom*.